JAKEMAN

Deborah Ellis

Fitzhenry & Whiteside

Text copyright © 2007 by Deborah Ellis

Published in Canada by Fitzhenry & Whiteside,
195 Allstate Parkway, Markham, Ontario L3R 4T8

Published in the United States by Fitzhenry & Whiteside,
311 Washington Street, Brighton, Massachusetts 02135

First published in paperback in the United States in 2008

www.fitzhenry.ca   godwit@fitzhenry.ca

10 9 8 7 6 5 4 3

Library and Archives Canada Cataloguing in Publication

Ellis, Deborah, 1960-
Jakeman / Deborah Ellis.
ISBN 978-1-55041-573-5 (bound)   ISBN 978-1-55041-575-9 (pbk.)
1. Children of women prisoners—Juvenile fiction. 2. Mothers and sons—Juvenile fiction. I. Title.
PS8559.L5494J33 2007   jC813'.54   C2006-906869-0

U.S. Publisher Cataloging-in-Publication Data
(Library of Congress Standards)

Ellis Deborah.
Jakeman / Deborah Ellis.
[192] p. : cm.
Summary: Jake and his older sister Shoshona, along with a busload of kids, visit their mother in prison regularly. But this time the journey turns into a series of misadventures, and the kids find themselves on their own, hatching a plan to find the Governor and plead with him to pardon their moms.
ISBN-10: ISBN 1-55041-573-5   ISBN-13: 9781550415735
ISBN-10: 1-55041-575-1 (pbk.)   ISBN-13: 9781550415759 (pbk.)
1. Children of women prisoners—Juvenile fiction.
2. Mothers and sons—Juvenile fiction. I. Title.
[Fic] dc22   PZ7.E4557 2007

Fitzhenry & Whiteside acknowledges with thanks the Canada Council for the Arts, and the Ontario Arts Council for their support of our publishing program. We acknowledge the financial support of the Government of Canada through the Book Publishing Industry Development Program (BPIDP) for our publishing activities.

Canada Council   Conseil des Arts
for the Arts   du Canada

ONTARIO ARTS COUNCIL
CONSEIL DES ARTS DE L'ONTARIO

Design by Wycliffe Smith
Printed in Canada

To the children of those we keep in cages

D.E.

Dear Mr. Governor,

We learned how to write letters at school. My teacher says you can pardon people out of prison. She says a lot of things, so I checked with Rawlins, who teaches me art at the Boys and Girls Club and has no reason to lie to me. He says it's true, so could you please pardon my mother, Shanice Kiera DeShawn. She's very nice and she didn't do anything wrong and if she did I know she's sorry.

Respectfully yours,

Jacob Tyronne DeShawn

P.S. Write me back. Let me know when she's coming back so I can be ready.

CHAPTER 1

The mighty Jakeman stalked the Queen of Pain through the dark and dreary city. Dangers waited in every shadow, but Jakeman was not afraid. The barbed wire under his skin would protect him. Jakeman's powers were greater than—

"Quit dragging your feet!"

Jake was too wet and tired to even bother to make a face at his sister's back. "I'm not dragging. You're walking too fast."

"You want to be late? You want to miss the bus?"

"You know I don't want to miss the bus. Why do you ask questions like that?" He half-ran a couple of steps to catch up.

Shoshona got off his back for all of ten seconds, then, "You still have the bag?"

Jake swung the big shopping bag at the back of her legs. "Course I still got the bag. You think I threw it in an alley? You think I sold it to somebody for a million dollars?"

"You complained about it enough. Why should I trust you?"

"I don't complain about the bag. I complain about the suit. Nobody else wears a suit."

"You think our mother's not good enough for a suit?"

That wasn't what he was thinking, and she knew it. "I'll put you in the bag," he muttered. The mighty Jakeman would fold up the Queen of Pain, tuck her away in the shopping bag, and have a nice, peaceful ride upstate. Jake, however, had to be content with swinging the bag at her legs again and hustling to keep up. He kept his free hand on the strap of his backpack, which was full of notebooks, drawing books, and stuff he didn't want stolen.

It was late, after midnight, and cold for a Mother's Day weekend. The thunder and lightning added to the craziness of the streets. Jake kept his head down to keep the rain off his face, and hung in behind his sister. At sixteen, she was five years older than he was and tall enough to act as a windbreak.

Jake didn't have to watch where they were going. Shoshona knew the way. She claimed to know everything. But it was harder than they expected to sneak out of their new foster parents' place, and that made them late.

"Why don't we just tell them we want to go?" Jake had asked. "They might even drive us to the bus."

"And if they say we can't go?" Shoshona had replied. "We'd have to disobey them and get off on another wrong foot. Do you want to start deciding things?"

So they snuck out with their backpacks and the shopping bag. There wasn't time to meet the others at the St. Jude's Community Center, where there would have been snacks and a place to wait before they headed out to the rain and the night crazies. Instead, Jake and his sister hurried right to the bus stop, Shoshona nagging him every two steps. When she wasn't nagging, she was humming one of those opera songs of hers, just to bug him more.

The humming stopped. "Hurry up. There's a line already."

"Is Harlan there?" Jake had to know so he could be prepared.

"Look for yourself."

He stepped out from behind his sister and got a face full of rain. But he was able to see the line of kids half a block away, stretched out under the narrow awning of the all-night drugstore. Some of the kids he would know—they were regulars, like him—and some would be strangers. There were always first-timers. Jake looked up and down the line. Even from this distance, Jake could be sure. Harlan wasn't there.

"He didn't come this time," Jake said.

"He doesn't scare me," said Shoshona.

"Easy to say that when he's not around." As they waited for the Walk sign, Jake could see Ms. Granite, the social worker who always took them on the bus. He also spotted someone who was almost as scary as Harlan, but in another way. Gitana. He'd recognize her hair anywhere, the way it curled and sprang away from her shoulders, like it might take off on its own at any moment.

Jake and Shoshona joined the line at the far end, where there was still a little room under the drugstore awning. If they stood flat against the display window, the rain couldn't get them.

"Who are you?" Two older girls—one with blonde hair pulled back into a ponytail and the other with a splash of freckles across her nose—appeared in front of them. Ponytail had a clipboard.

"Who are *you*?" Shoshona asked in return.

"I'm Janice," said the one with the clipboard. "On student placement with St. Jude's. This is Tina. We're helping Ms. Granite tonight. Are you going to Wickham?"

"Shoshona and Jake DeShawn," said Shoshona. She was good at answering only what she wanted to. Janice and Tina frowned at the sheet on the clipboard. "DeShawn. Is that one word or two?" Janice found the name and then asked, "Why didn't you meet us at the community center?"

"We're here now," said Shoshona.

"Can I have your clipboard?" asked Jake.

Janice did a funny sort of a fan-dance move with the clipboard. She pulled it close to her chest and stepped back, as if she thought Jake would reach out and grab it from her. Then she looked a little ashamed of herself and appeared to be actually thinking of handing it over. Then she gave herself a break and pushed Tina back down the line to bother some other kid.

Jake didn't really think she'd give him the clipboard, but it didn't hurt to try. He wanted it to hold his drawings.

There was nothing to do but wait. They did a lot of that on bus days. When it wasn't raining, Jake could draw, but he couldn't do anything in the rain.

Jake was tired and his feet were wet through his running shoes. He leaned against the window and gently bounced his head on the glass, just for something to do.

Slam! Something hit the other side of the glass. Jake turned around. The store clerks putting up the window display waved at him to back off. Jake was about to do something rude back at them when a kid came zooming up to him.

"*Bam!*" said the kid. "Jake the Man! Ready for a trip?"

"Dayton," said Jake. Jake the Man was his nickname at school. Dayton was in his class, the only one who hadn't laughed at his barbed-wire report. "I didn't know you had someone at Wickham."

"My mom," said Dayton. "She was someplace else.

They kept moving her, but we tracked her down. This should be fun. I never get to go anywhere. What are you doing?"

"Bugging these guys," he said, pointing at the clerks. "Check this out." He pulled his lips wide and stuck his tongue out at them. Dayton did something gross with his eyes.

The clerks tried to ignore them, but Jake banged on the window to make sure they paid attention. Shoshona took a few steps away so she could pretend she didn't know them. The clerks kept decorating the window, draping garlands of fake flowers over a stack of adult diapers for a Fun in the Sun display, until they got fed up and left.

"Some people don't know how to have fun," Dayton said.

"And some people don't know how to behave," said Shoshona.

"Who's that?" asked Dayton.

"Queen of Pain," Jake replied, turning his back to her. "Sister."

Dayton made one of his uglier faces and jerked his thumb down toward the other end of the line. "Mine's down there."

Jake stuck his neck out into the rain to look, just as the drugstore manager stormed out, waving his arms like he was on fire.

"Get away from my window! I'll call the cops!"

Ms. Granite stepped out of the line and into the rain. "I'm the social worker in charge of these children."

"Your kids are harassing my staff and blocking my customers."

Jake and Shoshona and everyone else looked toward the door. The last kid in line was at least ten feet away. No one was blocking anything.

"You know we're waiting for a bus," Ms. Granite said. "We've waited here before."

"And every time, there are complaints."

"From whom?"

The manager growled, "Just move those kids away from my store. They're scaring the customers. Your bus isn't going to drive up on the sidewalk. Wait out by the curb."

"It's raining."

"Is that my problem? Move it, or I'm calling the police."

Ms. Granite looked as if she might keep arguing.

But she gave it up and turned to face the lineup. "No sense fighting with fools. Move to the curb, children. Stick together."

"Too bad old Jakeman isn't here," said Dayton. He knew about Jakeman because Jake was always getting caught working on his comic book when he was supposed to be doing math or science. "He'd let them have it."

"Jakeman would smash the glass in the big window and throw the store people into the rain while we stood in the display case, warm and dry," Jake said. But Jakeman wasn't there, and Jake had to join the others along the curb, getting soaked by the rain and splashed by cars. Eons went by, until at last a battered old school bus pulled up. They could finally get the journey started.

Dear Mr. Governor,

They can't seem to find a place for us. We get to one foster home, and it's all, "He wets the bed. She argues too much. They don't fit in," and we're picked up again and put down someplace else. Each time we move, our bags are easier to carry because stuff gets stolen. Most of Mom's stuff is gone. I hope she blames Shoshona and not me.

Everyone says, "Yes, we'll send on your mail." But I haven't gotten any, so either they're lying or you haven't written me back yet. I know you're busy, but my teacher says you have staff to help you, so I don't know why you're taking so long.

I told Shoshona I was writing to you. She says you won't do anything, but she doesn't know as much as she thinks she does.

Our mother's name, in case you've forgotten, is Shanice Kiera DeShawn. Pardon her out of prison, and let me be smarter than my sister, just this once!

I'm probably making you think Shoshona is terrible, so maybe you think we're all terrible, but we're not, not even Shoshona. Mom was taking night school courses to be someone who looks after people when they're sick— not a nurse, but like a nurse. Shoshona gets good grades and works part-time at a sandwich shop in our old neighborhood. She also likes to sing. She wants to be an opera singer and sing on stage at Lincoln Center—she has a big enough mouth for it! (joke) And I'm going to be a famous comic-book artist. So, let Mom out of prison, Shoshona will sing you a song, and I will make you a hero in one of my comic books. And when you get old and sick, Mom will look after you.

Respectfully yours,

Jacob Tyronne DeShawn

A giant mountain of a man stepped out of the bus. He was so tall he had to duck his head to fit through the door.

"You're not our usual driver," said Jake.

"Get in the bus," the giant said.

"Our usual driver is Mr. Michaels. He's darker than me, and you're—"

"Paste," Dayton said. "You look like school paste."

"Shut up and get on the bus," the driver said.

"Why are you driving us tonight?" Jake asked. "Where's Mr. Michaels?"

"If you have to know, Michaels has the flu, and my friend who was supposed to fill in for him has a wife about to have a baby. I'm doing a favor for my friend, so don't give me any trouble."

"Is Mr. Michaels going to be okay? We like him," said Jake. "What do we call you?"

"Nothing," said the driver. "Don't talk to me."

"Okay, Mr. Nothing," said Jake. The other kids laughed.

"Only three of you to watch all these kids?" the driver asked Ms. Granite.

"I was supposed to have four students instead of two, but you know how that goes," Ms. Granite told him. "Anyway, it's late. They'll sleep most of the way."

"All I'm being paid to do is drive," Mr. Nothing said. "The brats are your problem."

"It's going to be a long night," Ms. Granite said to Janice and Tina, as they climbed up the steps. "Let's get them settled."

Jake got a seat to himself—behind Shoshona and in front of Dayton. His seat was torn, but at least he didn't have to share. The ten-hour bus ride was uncomfortable enough even when he could spread out a little. It was absolutely horrible when he had to sit up all night, squished and cramped.

"Stinks in here," said Dayton.

"It's worse than the last time," said Jake. The floor was sticky and gritty, and old chewing gum was everywhere. "Shoshona's taking driver's ed. When she gets her license and I sell my comic book, we'll get a car and drive up in comfort."

"Can I ride with you?" Dayton asked. "Me and my sister?"

"Plenty of room," Jake said. "It will be a big car."

Jake opened his backpack to look for his comic-book notebook. He wanted to jot down the window-smashing idea. As he groped through the bag, his hands brushed the leather case of his illegal drawing pens—illegal because he'd shoplifted them from the art supply store. They were fine, important pens, and he felt like a fine, important person when he used them. It was a whole drawing kit, with slim pens for slim lines, thicker pens for thick lines, and even charcoal for shading. One day when he was famous, he'd pay the store back. He'd made a personal sacred vow, but that wasn't the sort of thing Shoshona would understand. When she was around, the pens stayed out of sight.

There wasn't enough light in the bus for him to be able to tell which one was his art book, where he kept his work from his art lessons, his comic-book notebook, or the notebook full of rough copies of his letters to the governor. He was getting it sorted out when Shoshona turned around and asked, "You still have the bag?"

"Why do you keep bothering me? Of course I still have the—" Then he realized he didn't, and he had to jump off the bus to get it. The shopping bag was still on the sidewalk under the drugstore window. An old lady with a shopping cart piled high with junk was leaning down to go through it.

"Hey!" Jake yelled, to scare her away. She must have been used to people shouting at her because she didn't even jump. He had to snatch the bag right out of her hands. She made loud, police-siren noises and slapped her forehead over and over. Jake ran back to the bus as the other kids, who were pressed up at the windows, laughed.

"You did that on purpose," Shoshona said. Jake would have thrown the bag in her face, but it had their snacks in it as well as their change of clothes. He decided to keep it so she'd have to come begging to him when she got hungry. Not that Shoshona ever begged. She took or she went without.

Jake had just gotten settled into his seat again when

Ms. Granite started asking everyone about her brief-case. "Where did I put it? I'm sure it was right here."

Out of the corner of his eye, Jake saw Gitana lift the social worker's briefcase off the floor and tuck it under the pile of jackets and bags on her seat. She leaned against the pile and read the *New York Times* by the light of the streetlights outside—all casual and cool. The big, curly hair around her head glowed like a halo. Jake wondered if this was one of those special moments Rawlins was always telling him to watch out for. "Incandescent," Rawlins called them. "When the spirit of who the person really is can be seen and remembered and drawn." He'd have to ask Rawlins how real artists captured those moments. By the time he got his art book out of his backpack, the bus would be rolling and the moment would be over.

"Maybe I left it in the drugstore," Ms. Granite said. "Janice, don't let the bus leave without me." She dashed back into the drugstore in a panic.

"What have you got in your jacket?" Jake heard someone screech.

Tina, the student with freckles, was leaning over a seat, her eyes all white and wide. "I just saw your jacket move. What have you got in there?"

"That's my sister," Dayton said. "That's Carolyn. She doesn't talk. It drives people crazy."

Jake stood up to see, along with everybody else. Tina was opening and closing her mouth like a fish out of water, and spinning her head to look for rescue. She leaned over a small girl of seven. Carolyn had three ponytails in her hair and a completely blank look on her face. Ignoring Tina, she stared out the window.

By now, whatever was tucked inside Carolyn's jacket was getting tired of being cooped up. While everyone watched, the gray head of a cat popped out. It let out a great big *meow*.

Tina went ballistic. "Where did you get that? Did you steal that? You can't take a cat to prison!" On and on.

"It's just a cat," Gitana said.

"Yeah. Don't they teach about cats at your school?" Jake added, to show Gitana they were on the same side.

Carolyn kept perfectly still, as though she were waiting to have her picture taken. The cat kept meowing. The driver yelled that he wasn't driving any bus with a cat on it. Jake and the others—except for Shoshona, who'd stayed in her seat—laughed and made as big a deal out of it as they could. There wasn't anything else to entertain them.

Ms. Granite stepped back on the bus. "The clerks swear I didn't leave my briefcase in the store. It *must* be on the bus. We can't leave until I've found it." She saw the crowd around Carolyn, and the cat, and spoke sternly. "Carolyn, I thought we had an agreement that you wouldn't steal any more pets."

"It's probably a stray," said Clipboard Janice. "It doesn't have a collar."

The cat got tired of the grown-ups yelling and the children laughing. It worked its way out of Carolyn's jacket and made a mighty leap onto Tina.

Tina screamed and threw her arms in the air. The cat howled and jumped all over the bus, finally finding its way out the door and back onto the sidewalk.

Ms. Granite leaned over to lecture Carolyn. Jake saw Gitana put the briefcase back into the aisle.

"I'm hurt!" Tina cried. She had bleeding scratches on her face and hands. "I'm hurt!" she wailed, as though she'd been run through with a sword.

"Have you had a tetanus shot recently?" Ms. Granite asked.

"No! Do I need one?"

Ms. Granite said it was better to be safe, to get off the bus and get the shot first thing in the morning.

"Do I still get credit for this?" Tina asked. "I mean, I showed up like I was supposed to. This wasn't my fault." Then she backed up, tripping over the briefcase. Jake was laughing too much to hear Ms. Granite's answer. He didn't really care, anyway.

After that, everybody calmed down. The door was shut, and the driver steered the bus onto the street.

They were on their way.

But then the driver let out a big curse and slammed on the brakes. "What is *that*?"

The kids got up to look.

Standing in the rain, directly in front of the bus, was the kid Jake wanted most of all not to see. He was hunched into his old army jacket, the rain making his long, dark hair seem even longer and darker.

"He's with us," Ms. Granite said. "Let him on the bus."

"Who is it?" asked Dayton.

Lightning struck, lighting up the boy in the rain just like in a horror movie.

Jake said, "That's Harlan."

Dear Mr. Governor,

*I saw you on TV last night. It was kind of an acci-
dent, because our foster mother lets us watch only
nature shows and church shows. Sometimes they get
mixed up in my head, and I think the lion from the
nature show is going to get eaten by the preacher from
the church show, but he never does.*

*She was changing channels because she didn't like the
preacher who was on. He had a piece of fake hair on his
head and it flipped back when he got excited about the
Bible. She said it was hard to concentrate on God. She
changed channels with the remote because her legs are
bad from the diabetes.*

*She landed on the wrong channel, and there was you!
I knew it was you because it was written on the bottom.
You were with a bunch of kids playing baseball, and
everyone was smiling and looking all happy.*

*So I was thinking, maybe I could be one of those
kids! I could come to where you are, and we could play*

catch, and laugh a lot, and they could put it on TV, with me telling everyone what a great governor you are because you got my mom out of prison (Shanice Kiera DeShawn, hint, hint).

Don't you think that's a good idea? You could call me at my foster home, or at my school, and I'll be ready anytime.

Respectfully yours,

Jacob Tyronne DeShawn

The driver cursed and shouted, but the kids on the bus were used to cursing and shouting, so no one took much notice. He was no match for Ms. Granite anyway; she made him open the door so Harlan could get in.

Harlan squished his way up the steps and down the aisle, his shoes full of rain. Everyone slid into their seats so he could move without challenge. He was older. Maybe fifteen. He looked wet, hulking, dark, and angry.

Harlan headed toward the back of the bus. Jake thought he was going to keep going, but he stopped right by Jake's seat. He raised his head just enough for

Jake to see his eyes, cold and hard. Jake didn't wait for the order. He vacated the seat and Harlan moved into it.

Jake was quick enough to grab both the shopping bag and his backpack. He found another empty seat behind Dayton and sat down.

"Give him a towel," Shoshona said. When Jake didn't move, she got up, grabbed the shopping bag, found the towel, and held it out to Harlan. Harlan ignored it.

"Don't be a fool," Shoshona said. "Dry yourself."

Harlan glared at her hard and long. Shoshona kept the towel where it was, hanging off the end of her outstretched arm, and didn't back down. Harlan slowly reached out, took the towel, and wiped away the water from his face. Shoshona sat down in her own seat, without another word.

"What's with him?" Dayton whispered.

"He threw a fit during the Christmas visit," Jake whispered back. "I got in his way."

"Bet you didn't do that twice."

"He doesn't scare me," Jake said. He turned his face to the window to end the conversation.

The bus was all stop and start for the first hour or so, as it made its way through the city traffic. No one felt like talking. The bus was quiet except for the *swish-swish* of the window wipers.

Jake stared out the window. The lonely, tight feeling was already creeping over him—as it always did on prison weekends—and they still had a long way to go.

He fell asleep, off and on, when the bus got out onto the freeway and could roll along smoothly. His backpack was a pillow, all hard surfaces and edges. The shopping bag was a softer choice, but Shoshona would have a dozen fits if he wrinkled their good clothes with his tired head. He dozed with a sore neck and drool on his face.

"What are you doing?"

Jake woke up to the sound of Ms. Granite arguing with the driver.

"I'm stopping for breakfast." He was steering the bus onto a turn-off lane that led to a gas station restaurant.

"We usually stop at the McDonald's a few miles from the prison. The children will want to get cleaned up before seeing their mothers."

"I'm not stopping twice, and I need to eat now."

"But the children—"

"The children can stay on the bus or get off it and

lie down in traffic, for all I care." He brought the bus
to a stop, and turned around to yell at everyone.
"Thirty minutes. Be back here in half an hour. I'm not
waiting around or counting heads. I'm just being paid
to drive," he reminded Ms. Granite again.

Jake stumbled out to the parking lot with the others, all sleepy and bumping into things.

"Go back in and get the shopping bag," Shoshona
ordered him. "We'll change now."

"Now?"

"We might not get a chance later."

Jake went back in for the shopping bag.

"Wash," Shoshona ordered when they got inside.
"If you don't wash properly on your own, I'll drag you
into the ladies' room and wash you myself."

"You try and the barbed wire will come out of my
skin and you won't stand a chance," Jake said, low
under his breath. Shoshona had good hearing when she
wanted to.

Shoshona took her own clothes out of the shopping
bag and went into the ladies' room to change. Jake
went into the men's, squirted enough soap onto himself
to satisfy his sister, then got into his suit. Mom had
bought the suit from a secondhand shop a few months

before she was arrested. "You need a suit for church," she had said. "You'll grow into this one." That was three years ago. It still didn't fit. It was floppy and old-fashioned, and Jake hated it. He kept wishing it would get stolen like so much of his other stuff from his old life, but nobody was dumb enough to take it.

"What a loser," one of the boys from the bus said when Jake stepped out of the stall, freshly changed. "We're going to a prison, not a church. You look like a fool."

Jake used Shoshona's line. "Maybe your mother's just not good enough for you to put on a suit."

The other boy leapt at him, and there would have been a fight—and trouble from Shoshona for messing his clothes—but some old guy washing his hands threatened to call management if they didn't quit. The boys turned away from each other and told the man to mind his own business. By the time the man yelled back at them, dried his hands, and left, the moment had passed and no one felt like fighting anymore.

Jake put his jacket on over his suit and went out into the entranceway to wait with the others. Ms. Granite and Janice were keeping them together. Jake and Dayton tried to wander off to look at the video games in the little arcade, but Shoshona hauled them back to the group.

The foyer opened directly into the restaurant. Jake could see their driver shoveling eggs and bacon into his mouth with great speed. None of the kids had extra money for breakfast. Their money had to be saved for lunch at the prison.

"You know all these kids?" Dayton asked.

"Some," Jake said. "There's new kids every time. That's Gitana, with the newspaper. Those are the Hernandez brothers—the smaller one's Ricardo, the other is Manuel." He pointed to two younger boys, sitting on the floor by the door.

"What about them?" Dayton asked about three girls with long, bright feather boas around their necks. They were a little younger than Jake, and they were all giggling.

"That's Rochelle, Lydia, and Clarice. They're crazy. Don't even look at them. You'll set them off."

The gigglers either didn't hear or didn't care about Jake's opinion. They twirled their feather boas, practiced dance moves, and giggled harder when they messed up.

A couple of people stared as they entered the restaurant. They would stare anyway at such a big group of kids hanging out together. The dancers made it worse.

It got even worse when the three girls started to sing. They lined themselves up in a row, tilted their hips, pointed their fingers, and sang, "Jump! For my love!"

One pinched-faced woman carrying a whining baby snarled at them to get out of her way.

"You shouldn't even be singing that song," she said, interrupting the girls. "That's a Pointer Sisters song. One of you is white, and none of you can sing."

Lydia, the white Pointer Sister, started tossing the insults back, and was soon joined by Jake and everybody else, even though the girls had been annoying and embarrassing them just seconds before. Ms. Granite thought it would be a good idea for everyone to move outside. At least the rain had slowed to a drizzle.

The driver came out soon after. He walked right past the children as if they weren't there. The children followed him across the parking lot, like he was leading a parade.

Harlan was already on the bus. No one spoke to him, and he spoke to no one.

It was hard to get back to sleep. Jake started to nod off, felt himself falling, and jerked awake again. A few rows ahead of him, one of the Hernandez brothers started crying about something. He could hear Ms. Granite's soothing voice. He pretended she was talking to him, and that helped.

The next thing he knew, Ms. Granite had made the bus driver stop at the McDonald's for a quick bathroom break and another wash. Not long after that, they arrived at the prison.

Dear Mr. Governor,

Did you know that barbed wire used to be called Devil's rope?

Did you know that there are over two thousand types of barbed wire?

Did you know that the inventor of barbed wire was Joseph F. Gliddon? He was born in New York State! You could have been his governor, if you'd been around back then. It was originally invented for cattle. Now it's used for people.

There's even a museum of barbed wire. It's in Texas, though, not New York. Maybe you could ask the Texas governor to give it to us, since the inventor came from here.

(But pardon my mother first. Shanice Kiera DeShawn. You remember.)

The reason I know so much about barbed wire is I did a school project about it. The teacher said it could be about anything, but she really meant anything on her list. I didn't like her list so I got a bad mark and most of the class thought I was an idiot for choosing barbed wire, but it was actually very interesting.

Since I'm asking you to do a favor for me (pardoning my mom), I'm going to do a favor for you. I'm going to tell you about my superhero. His name is Jakeman, the Barbed Wire Boy. He looks like a regular kid, but he's not. If he's grabbed by bad guys, barbed wire comes out of his skin and the attackers get all bloody and sore. He's got other superpowers, too, like legs that grow long when he needs to run and arms that grow strong when he needs to fight. Rawlins, who teaches me art, is a real artist. People pay him to draw their portraits. He makes me do exercises like drawing hands over and over and Old Masters stuff, but he helps me with the comic book, too. If you let my mother out of jail, I'm sure Rawlins would paint a portrait of you to hang in your office. Then, when people come in to see you, they'll see two of you, and you'll look even more impor-tant.

So, that's actually two favors. I hope you like them, and I hope you write to me soon to say when Mom is coming home.

Don't steal my idea.

Respectfully yours,

Jacob Tyronne DeShawn

CHAPTER 4

The fence came first.

It rose out of an open field, like a crazy steel crop where there should have been corn and barley. Then there were the towers like treehouses, where guards played with loaded guns and giant lights like artificial sunflowers.

If a prisoner on the run could make it through the locked doors in the building and past the first and second fences, which carried enough electricity to kill small animals, there was still the third fence. Fifteen feet high, with no place for a foot to hang on, with two giant coils of razor wire running along the top, ready to slice. Another row of razor wire lined the bottom of each side of the fence.

This third fence also used to be electric, but deer and dogs and kids playing ball kept running into it. Wickham Correctional Institute for Women was in hunting territory. People didn't think it was a good idea to kill a deer with an electric fence. That's what double-barreled shotguns were for. So they took away the electric fence and brought in guards and razor wire.

"Is that it?" Dayton asked, coming to sit beside Jake.

"No. That's a candy store," Jake said, then felt bad and added, "There's a gate up ahead. That's where we'll go."

The prison fence seemed to go on forever. Behind it, they could see buildings, old and new, ugly and sad. Everyone automatically looked for their mother in the exercise yard, but the prisoners were all inside.

The driver pulled up to the curb along a narrow sidewalk beside the high brick wall of the administration building. He opened the door.

"Everybody out."

Ms. Granite jumped into action. "Visiting doesn't start for over two hours. You can't make these children just stand here. What if it starts raining again?"

"My job is to drive them here. Now I'm going to

get some sleep so I can drive them back. You don't want to get out? Fine with me. You can sit in the parking lot of the motel while I sleep."

Ms. Granite tried to argue that the other driver left the bus in the parking lot for them to wait in and took a cab to the motel, but Mr. Nothing didn't care. Everyone had to get out of the bus.

"Be careful what you take in with you," Shoshona said. "Remember the rules." She opened the shopping bag and took out the bundle of gifts they'd brought for their mother and the snacks she'd packed for breakfast. They left everything else on the bus.

Jake hated doing that. He didn't trust Mr. Nothing not to go through his stuff, but he trusted the prison guards even less. The backpack stayed behind. He joined his sister and the others on the sidewalk outside the visitors' entrance.

The food Shoshona had packed was nothing more than a hot dog bun each, spread with strawberry diet spread their foster mother kept around instead of jam. "I had to pack in secret," she said, when Jake complained. "You know how they like to lock up the good stuff." The bun was stale and the spread tasted like nothing, but Jake ate it anyway. The other kids finished off their bag lunches from the community center. It was something to do.

"Put your trash in the bin," Ms. Granite reminded them all. "We don't want to give the guards a reason to get upset."

After that, there was nothing to do, not even drawing to pass the time.

"How long do they make us wait?" Dayton asked.

"Until they're ready."

"I hate waiting."

"You'll get used to it," Jake said, although he never did.

Gitana had brought a chunk of her newspaper with her off the bus and was reading it while she waited. Jake saw a face he recognized on the front page.

Now he could really impress her. "That's the governor," he said. "Did you know that's the governor?"

"Of course," she said. She turned over the newspaper so she could see the article. Jake moved closer to peer over her shoulder. Her hair smelled like rain and coconuts. She pointed at the other photos. "And that's the president, and that's a senator."

"What's the governor in the paper for?" Jake asked. He didn't care about the other guys. He'd never written to them. "Who's that old lady in the picture with him?"

"That old lady is his mother. It's an article about where they're spending Mother's Day, and go buy your own paper." She stamped her foot down almost on top of Jake's.

"I don't need to read about it in the newspaper," Jake said. "He'll probably tell me all about it in his next letter."

Gitana lowered her paper. "The governor writes to you?"

"Oh sure. We send letters back and forth all the time." With that, he turned and went back to his old spot in the line. He wanted to leave her impressed but without a chance to ask questions. Also, she was standing a little too close to Harlan's end of the line for his comfort.

She almost stomped on my foot, he thought. It was a glorious moment.

Dayton came over to him. He put his face real close to Jake's ear. Jake was about to give him a big shove when Dayton whispered, "Are you sure they'll let us out again?"

"You've never done this before? You've never been to a prison before?"

Dayton shook his head.

Jake was an expert. "They'll let us out. They don't want to let us in. It disrupts their day."

Once Jake spoke, other repeaters had to put their two cents in.

"I hope you're wearing good underwear because the guards might strip-search you, and they'll laugh if it's all torn."

"They listen in on your conversations, so don't confess to any crimes."

"If you break even just one rule, they'll throw you out."

Jake and the others kept it up for a while. It broke up the boredom. Dayton and the other new kids looked more and more scared.

Finally, Jake took pity and pulled Dayton out of line. "There are lots of rules, but they're all written on the walls. There are lots of guards, but just do what they tell you to do, and don't answer back, no matter how stupid it sounds."

And then Dayton asked the question that was really bothering him. He asked, "What if she doesn't recognize me?"

Jake had to bluff an answer to that one. He had

scared his friend enough. "Don't be an idiot. She's your mother. Of course she'll recognize you. How long since you've seen her?"

"A year."

Jake turned away. He couldn't bluff that much. His own rule was that a month could go by, and no problem. He'd heard of kids going away to camp for a month, but he'd never heard of their parents not recognizing them when they got home. Beyond a month, he could never be sure, and there was always at least three months between visits. It was always scary, waiting to see if Mom remembered him.

The waiting continued. It started to rain again. Other people joined the line, leaving their cars in the parking lot and lining up by themselves or with their kids. Everyone waited and waited and waited.

At last, the guards appeared. They were laughing with each other, as if what was about to happen was no big deal. One of the guards went into his speech.

"We will have order! We're letting you in early because of the rain, but you will not push. You will not shove. You will be searched. Any violations of the rules will result in your visit being terminated, and any future visits will be put at risk. Your visit will be monitored. Any exchange of contraband will result in criminal charges being brought against you and the inmate you are visiting."

He barked on and on. Finally they were let in through the first gate. Jake stuck close to Shoshona, who showed their ID. Their names were checked against a list, and they were allowed to go through to the building.

The entrance to the visitors' room was like a long cage, with high fences on either side of the walkway, and razor wire curled around the top. Where there wasn't razor wire, there was barbed wire, strand after long strand of it. Jake was always afraid all this wire would fall on him and he'd be cut into millions of tiny pieces.

"Don't like barbed wire, boy?" a guard asked, seeing Jake cringe. "Better get used to it. You'll probably spend your whole life looking through it."

Jakeman would have used his huge arm muscles to fling the guard in the air and leave him hanging on the razor wire, his legs kicking and birds landing on his screaming head.

Jake just shut his ears and kept moving.

Finally, the doors closed behind them, and they were in prison.

Dear Mr. Governor,

You need to build a bathroom by the prison in case people have to go while they're waiting to visit. It doesn't have to be fancy. I counted six portable toilets at a building site near my school. You could move one to the prison and the builders would still have five. Then little kids could go in there and not against the prison wall if they can't hold it in. Then the guards wouldn't yell about property damage, and visits wouldn't be canceled.

You can do this and pardon my mother.

Respectfully yours,

Jacob Tyronne DeShawn

*J*ake stood a little behind his sister. The counter in front of him came up to his nose. On his first visit, it was at the top of his forehead. He'd grown a little bit, but there was still plenty of room in his suit. He'd be wearing that ugly old thing until he was ninety.

Shoshona passed up their ID again. The guard frowned and scratched himself.

"This is Jacob?" he asked.

"Yes," said Shoshona.

"What's your name?" he barked at Jake.

Calvin Coolidge, thought Jake. "Jake. Jacob."

The guard looked at Jake as if he was a worm that had just crawled out of his butt, then handed Shoshona back the papers and waved them through.

The line moved slowly. The people ahead of Jake and Shoshona were searched. They were crowded with the others in a narrow hallway—waiting, waiting, waiting again.

"It's like that cattle ranching video we saw at school," Dayton said. He and Carolyn were right behind Jake. "We're all cows at the gate, waiting for the cowboys to let us into the next pen."

"Mooo," said Jake. Dayton laughed. The guards snarled. Shoshona elbowed Jake in the ribs to shut him up.

Behind them, Harlan came up to the front counter. Ms. Granite was with him. Jake nudged Dayton to watch.

"Who are you here to see?" the guard asked Harlan.

Harlan took a photo out of his army jacket pocket and put it on the counter, under the guard's nose. "My mother. Marion Falconer," he said. "Only I can't because you killed her."

The guard looked up in surprise, then said, "Oh. You again. Are you going to give me problems this time? Because visiting is a privilege, buddy, it's not a right."

"He's here to see his aunt, Sandra Haldimand," Ms. Granite said. She had the same talent as Shoshona for redirecting the conversation.

"My mother said she was sick, but you didn't believe her," Harlan said. "She asked for a doctor, and you didn't get her one."

"I told you not to start with me." The guard passed the photo back to Harlan. "I don't even work in that part of the prison."

"I deserve an apology," Harlan said. "My mother deserves an apology."

That got the guard mad. "I don't have to apologize to you or to anyone, and certainly not to some dead prisoner. I don't know how your mother died or why, but it was nothing to do with me, and my union will back that up, so just shut your mouth. Move him along," he said to Ms. Granite, then, back at Harlan, "You step out of line again, you even look like you're going to raise your voice, and you'll get a quick trip to juvenile hall. It's where you'll end up anyway, on your way to death row." He looked over to the other guards. "This one's a crime waiting to happen," he said, and they laughed.

"Is this necessary?" Ms. Granite asked.

"Yes, after the last time, it's completely necessary. We've been ordered to cooperate with children's services, but we're running a prison, not a mental hospital."

"Then what are *you* doing here?" Gitana asked.

Jake slapped a hand over his mouth so he wouldn't laugh. The guard pretended he hadn't heard.

"They killed his mother?" Dayton whispered, his eyes wide and scared. "That can happen?"

"No talking!" yelled a guard.

Jake waited until the guard turned away. Then he whispered quickly, "Don't worry. Your mom is fine." He turned away quickly, too, so Dayton couldn't press him for more.

The line moved ahead.

"Empty your pockets," the searching guard ordered Jake. All the searching guards wore tight, white rubber gloves, so they wouldn't catch any germs from the kids. "No keys, no pens, no weapons or anything that could be used as a weapon. No paper money. Coins only."

Jake emptied his pockets. There wasn't much there, just the Kleenex Shoshona always made him carry. All the good stuff was back in his jeans pockets, in the shopping bag, on the bus.

"Raise your arms."

Jake stuck his arms out straight from his shoulders. The guard waved a metal detector wand up and down his body.

"Turn around."

Jake did what he was told. The wand reached his left butt cheek and started to beep.

"You were told to empty your pockets."

"I did!" Jake put his hand back there and realized he'd forgotten something. He took it out. It was a slug—a round, flat piece of metal about the size of a quarter. "I found it on the way home from church last Sunday," he told Shoshona. "I forgot I had it."

"You were going to try to put this in one of the vending machines," the guard accused. "You were going to try to steal from the State of New York."

"No, no. I..." Jake couldn't say what he'd planned to do with it, because he hadn't planned anything. It was just too good a thing to leave in the street.

"Do you want this visit to go forward?" the guard snarled. "Do you want us to arrest you for trying to smuggle contraband into the prison? Do you want to spend the night in juvenile detention?"

Jake wanted to answer one yes and two no's, but

he wasn't sure the guard would match the right answer to the right question.

"I'm sure my brother didn't mean anything," Shoshona said. "He's just very forgetful. He doesn't think when he should."

Jake wanted to hit her, but he held his temper.

"Shoes and socks," he was told. Jake had to show the bottom of his feet and be prodded between his toes. Then, with everybody watching, he had to take off his jacket and tie and shirt. He tried to puff up his chest so it wouldn't seem so skinny. It was cold in the prison, and he shivered.

"Maybe next time you'll remember," the guard said, waving him on.

Don't you want to see my butt? Jake wanted to ask. *I've got good underwear on today. I don't care if you see my butt.* But he held his tongue and put his shirt back on.

"Your tie is crooked," Shoshona said, slapping his hands away and retying it herself. Jake could see Gitana looking at him, and turned away in shame.

A guard started to take apart the gift parcel Shoshona and Jake had brought for their mother.

"White socks only," he said, holding up the socks

Jake had chosen. They were all white except for a little bit of blue thread at the top. Jake thought they'd make a nice change from the usual.

"You never listen," Shoshona said. "I told you. Now Mom's feet will be cold."

Jake didn't want his mother to have cold feet. "Can't you just cut the tops off?" he asked, but the guard had already tossed the contraband socks onto the floor behind the table, like they were garbage—not a gift that had been chosen and paid for.

The guard pawed through the whole package. Jake and Shoshona could give their mother three packages a year. As soon as they delivered one, they began saving up for another. Jake knew the approved list by heart: two bars of white, unscented soap; roll-on deodorant; white underwear and socks; two dozen white envelopes; two tubes of toothpaste. The guard always squeezed a little out of each tube to be sure it was toothpaste. They could also give Mom a small plastic jar of instant coffee, twenty tea bags, six packets of dried soup, and a small bag of hard candy. They always got her everything that was on the list. Whatever she didn't need herself, she traded for other things.

59

The guard wrapped up the package again and set it aside. Mom would get it after the visit. "Sit," the guard said.

Jake followed Shoshona into the visiting room and took a seat on the long bench by the wall. The room was all gray walls, gray metal tables, and gray benches bolted to the gray floor. No pictures on the walls, just big signs full of rules in English and Spanish. The only color came from the vending machines and the wide yellow line that prisoners weren't allowed to cross.

"No talking!" yelled a guard, even though no one was talking.

More and more waiting. Jake wished he had his notebook.

"Do you want to see what I have?"

He looked up and saw a little girl standing in front of him. She was maybe four years old, all dressed up in a party dress with her hair full of ribbons. She put her hand on his knee.

"Do you want to see what I have?" she asked again.

Jake glanced at the guard. He didn't want anybody yelling at this little kid for talking. He nodded at the girl.

She took a little purse out of her pocket and slowly counted out coins. "I'm going to buy Mommy a chocolate bar," she said. "I've been saving."

"She'll like that," Jake told her quietly. He helped her put the coins back in her purse so she wouldn't drop them.

"I'm Sophie," she said.

"I'm Jake."

"You look like the man on the cake," she said. "Will you marry me?"

Even the guards started to laugh. Jake wanted to fall through the floor, but it was concrete, so he had to sit where he was. He tried to think of a Jakeman super-power that would get him out of it, but nothing came into his head. It hurt to try to think without being able to draw.

He was rescued by a tall, thin man with a full head of long dreadlocks. The man picked up Sophie and said, "I'm a baker. I specialize in wedding cakes. Sophie is my daughter."

Jake was about to say he wasn't anywhere near wanting to get married, but the guard went into his no-talking routine again, and he was left alone.

Waiting, waiting, waiting. The benches filled up. It

was getting close to the time when Mom would walk into the room.

Jake jumped at every yelp from the guards, looked up at the clock forty times a minute, and stared at the door to the prison, wishing he had the superpower to make it open. The little kids started to fuss.

Finally, he heard it. The *slap-slap* noise of flip-flops on the concrete floors. The prisoners were coming. His mother was coming. She was real close. She was just on the other side of the door.

Dear Mr. Governor,

Maybe you don't like your mother. Maybe you got stuck with a real nasty mother, so you think they're all that way, and should all be in jail. Maybe that's why you haven't written me back, and maybe that's why my mother is still in prison.

You should meet my mother. You should come to Wickham when Shoshona and I are there. That way, you can meet all of us. We'll buy you lunch from the vending machines. Anything you want!

My foster parents are okay. It's nice to have a dad—even a foster one—to help me with my homework and take me to buy shoes. And our foster mom says nice things when we get home from school and asks about our day and gives us a snack. But it's not the same. We're not really living there. We're just visiting. One day, they'll get tired of us, and Ms. Granite or some other worker will pick us up and say, "This next place will work out just fine." And we'll start all over again.

63

With Mom, we wouldn't be visiting, we'd be living. She'd think of things to ask me that my foster parents don't because they don't know me. And from the time I was a little baby, she always sang me to sleep. She sang "America the Beautiful" because she wanted us to go to sleep always remembering that this country is just as much ours as it is anybody's. She didn't sing it like a march, though, like they do on TV, and she didn't sing it all bored, like we do at school. She sang it like a prayer. We'd sing it with her sometimes, and add harmonies. Shoshona's good at making up harmonies. And when we sang it, even if I'd had a lousy day, it made me believe that the next day would be better.

Shoshona tried to sing it to me when Mom was first taken away, but it didn't sound right, so I asked her to stop. She sings one of her church songs instead, or one of her opera songs—a quiet one, not squealy. It helps, but it's not Mom.

So, please come to Wickham and meet us. Then you'll see that we're good people, and deserve to be happy.

Respectfully yours,

Jacob Tyronne DeShawn

CHAPTER 6

One at a time, the prisoners were announced. The guard yelled out the names. "Bottsworth!" "Juarez!" "Carmichael!" Every time the guard opened his mouth, Jake rose a little off the bench. Gitana shouted, "Gran!" and ran across the room to hug a woman with white hair and a smile on her wrinkled face. They both looked happy, and Jake felt good.

Then Sophie dashed across the room to a woman who was already on her knees, arms spread wide open. Sophie almost ran right into the woman's arms, then she stopped like she'd smacked against a wall. She turned to her father, her fingers in her mouth, all scared. He knelt down and talked to her, real soft and gentle. Jake couldn't hear the words, but knew her father was saying, "It's okay, this really is your mama, everything's all right." Jake liked that the man was nice and gentle and didn't hit her for being afraid. Inch by inch, party-dress Sophie moved forward, until she was inside those spread-out arms, and those arms were all around her.

An *incandescent* moment. Jake heard the word in his head in just the same musical way Rawlins would say it.

"Holmes!" Jake saw Dayton and Carolyn stand up. Dayton held his sister's hand and tried to smooth out their clothes so they looked nice. A woman ran toward them, crying, but with a big smile on her face. Dayton and Carolyn were frozen.

Their mother stopped right in front of them, just the other side of the wide, yellow line on the floor. "Oh, my babies," she cried.

They still didn't move. Jake stood up. "She can't cross the line," he said to Dayton. "You have to go the rest of the way." He gave them a push, to get their legs started. Then they were with their mother and everything was all right.

Jake sat down again. "Beginners," he said to Shoshona.

"DeShawn!" the guard yelled out.

Jake felt himself go hot and cold. His heart beat like crazy. He wanted to laugh and dance and cry and hide. Finally, through the doors came his mother. It didn't even take half a second for him to know that she still remembered him.

"You're wearing my sweater."

After all the excited hellos and I-love-yous were over, the awkward time settled in. Sometimes Mom was feeling happy, and the visit was easy, but not always. This time, Jake, Shoshona, and Mom sat around one of the gray metal tables as if they were strangers. Between visits, Jake thought of all sorts of things to tell her. But when he got into that gray room, his brain went dull.

Mom was the first one to break the silence, and that's when she said it.

"You're wearing my sweater."

Shoshona was. It was light purple, with buttons that shimmered like pearls. Jake couldn't tell if Mom was angry or not.

"I remember seeing that sweater in the store window and saving up for it a little out of each paycheck."

Shoshona touched one of the buttons. "I don't wear it for everyday," she said. "Just for special." Her voice was weak and un-bossy.

"Your father liked me in that sweater."

Jake had never met his dad. He left just before Jake was born. No one knew where he was. When he was younger, Jake thought his dad was on the International Space Station, but he knew a lot of kids whose fathers had also left home. They couldn't all be on the Space Station.

"Now you're wearing it and walking in the world, and I'm in here, wearing orange." All the prisoners in Wickham wore orange jumpsuits.

"I take good care of it," Shoshona said. "I'll put it away for you, if you want me to."

"No. Wear it. What does it matter?" Jake couldn't tell if she meant it or not.

"I just hope you appreciate your freedom," Mom said. "I just hope and pray that every day, you are grateful for being out in the world and not stuck behind these walls like your mother. Do you appreciate it?"

Shoshona and Jake both said yes, then looked down

at their hands again. They had to keep their hands on top of the table. It was one of the rules, written up on a big sign: Hands On Top of the Table At All Times.

"Look at your nails," Mom said to Jake. He'd missed a few lines of dirt. Shoshona kicked him. "Isn't your sister taking proper care of you?"

"I take care of myself," Jake said. He curled his fingers into his palms. There was no way to hide his hands.

"He's growing up," Shoshona said. "It's getting harder and harder to make him do what I tell him."

"You mind your sister," Mom said to Jake. "I know you've got all these foster parents and social workers and youth workers and all, but Shoshona's the boss. I don't want to hear about you misbehaving."

Jake squirmed. *What are you going to do about it? You can't even tell yourself what to do.* He didn't like to think those kinds of thoughts. They made him feel mean and small.

Instead, he said, "I got a good mark on my geography test. It was a test about rivers—where they go, how long they are, and like that. I'll send it to you when I get it back. My teacher put it up on the bulletin board to show everyone on parent-teacher night."

Shoshona kicked him again. Too late he realized he'd said something that could make Mom sad, make her think of other parents getting to look at Jake's test paper while she was stuck in prison.

"Tell her about your math test," Shoshona said. "Tell her about skipping school. Tell her about that fight you got into."

"It wasn't a fight!" Jake had been showing off one of Jakeman's superpower moves—the one where his legs grow three times their normal size. He'd been running across the playground on those big legs, when he'd bumped into someone by accident, and one thing had led to another.

"What do you expect me to do from here?" Mom asked. "He's your brother. He's your responsibility."

"I try, but—"

"Just like my being in here is your responsibility, too."

Jake's breath stopped. Sometimes she was bitter, and sometimes she was sad, but he had never before heard his mother say such a thing.

"You both kept asking for stuff," Mom said. "You wanted singing lessons and science camp, video games, paints, and other art supplies. Fancy running shoes.

How was I supposed to pay for all that? I could barely pay my night-school fees."

"I wasn't..." Shoshona tried again. "I didn't...I was just dreaming. Just talking and dreaming."

"I had to find someone to help me," Mom said. "That's when I went out and met Rodney."

Rodney was Mom's boyfriend.

Jake watched Shoshona's normally iron face crumble like a stale cookie.

"We never asked you to—," began Shoshona.

"No," Mom said. "You never asked me to. And when I did, you didn't appreciate it. He offered to pay for those singing lessons for you, and you wouldn't let him."

Jake's memory of Rodney was of a long man, a man so long his feet hung off the end of the sofa. He had long arms, too, and they'd fly around, slapping and slugging when he had too much to drink or Jake made too much noise. He carried a big roll of bills in his pocket and peeled them off like he was peeling an orange. Jake hadn't liked him. Shoshona had hated him.

"And now you're out there, wearing my sweater, while I'm in here, wearing orange."

Jake looked at the clock hung high up on the wall.

There was still ages to go. Everything went quiet again.

"Rodney's out," Shoshona said abruptly. "I saw him in our old neighborhood."

Jake let out a yelp but clamped his hand quickly over his mouth. Loud noises weren't allowed in the visiting room.

"Did you hear what I said? Rodney's out. He's out of prison." Shoshona's voice got a bit of its bossiness back.

"Watch your tone," Mom said.

"If he's out, you should be out. You said they were his drugs. You said you didn't know they were there. If he's out, you should be out."

"He spoke against me to the DA," Mom said. "I loved him, and he said all that cocaine was mine, that I'd brought it into our apartment without telling him. I loved him and he did that to me." She started to cry.

Shoshona kept on. "But it wasn't yours. You can prove it. Didn't they ask you how you got it? Didn't your lawyer help you?"

Mom wiped her eyes on the sleeve of her jumpsuit. "When Rodney said all those things, it was like the lights went out. We were going to have a home. Remember when we talked about that? Maybe a little house in another neighborhood. He was going to take care of me. Then he said those things. The DA made my lawyer an offer. My lawyer told me to take it."

"And you took it?" Shoshona asked.

"What else could I have done?"

"You could have fought them! You could fight them now!"

Jake's palms were sweaty. He wiped them on the thighs of his trousers.

"Hands!" yelled the guard, zooming over to the table. Jake yanked his hands back to the tabletop.

"You see that sign?" The guard bent over him, puffing bad breath in his face. "Do you know how to read? Does he know how to read?" he asked Shoshona.

"He can read. He just made a mistake."

"Hands on top of the table at all times! I'll be watching you. You do it again, this visit is terminated."

The guard stepped back. Jake saw all the other kids in the room flatten their hands on the tabletop.

Jake's table fell silent again. No one felt like arguing anymore.

In the little pocket of quiet, Jake's stomach rumbled. That made the three of them laugh. It wasn't really funny. They just needed to laugh.

Shoshona held up her coin purse. "Let's get ourselves a feast!" she said.

Mom held Jake's hand on the way to the vending machines. It felt familiar and safe—the sort of hand that would keep him out of traffic and away from monsters.

Ms. Granite waved hello as he walked by. She and Janice were sitting on the long bench, eating sandwiches from the vending machines and writing things in files. He waved back with his free hand and even smiled a little. With his mom by his side, he felt good. He felt normal. Besides, Ms. Granite was okay.

They got to the machines.

"I want a Coke," Jake said.

"You'll have tomato juice," his mother said, like he knew she would. "I'll have one, too."

Mom wasn't allowed to handle money. She also had to stay behind the yellow line. Jake stood with her while Shoshona put the coins in and handed over three tins of tomato juice and three little cardboard trays of nachos with cheese sauce.

"This is my boyfriend," party-dress Sophie said, coming over to the machines with her mother. "We're going to be married and stand at the top of a cake."

"It will have to be a big cake," Sophie's mother said, shaking Jake's hand as if he was a real person, not just a kid. "I'm Lavinia. Thank you for being so kind to my daughter."

"I'm Jake." He liked being thanked. He lifted Sophie up so she could put her coins in the chocolate bar machine. She chose a bar and pulled the lever.

Nothing happened.

"They raised the prices again," Shoshona said.

"I don't have enough money!" Sophie began to wail and wail, right in Jake's ear. He got another quarter from Shoshona and gave it to Sophie. Sophie's mother got her chocolate bar, and Jake was treated like a big hero by the small group of orange-clad women around the vending machines.

Jake and his family carried their food back to the table. It felt normal, to be sharing a meal. Mom wasn't crying anymore. They ate and laughed and talked about things that didn't matter.

"Are these your children?

Warden Scofield was upon them. She made an appearance during every visit. She always wore gray, like the room, and soft-soled shoes so she could sneak up on people.

"We met last time," Shoshona said. *And the time before that, and the time before that.*

"So many prisoners have so many children," Warden Scofield said. She smiled, but the smile didn't reach her eyes. "You don't visit often, do you?"

"Four times a year," Jake said.

"We live far away," Shoshona said.

"I guess you are busy with other things," the warden said. "Plus, this is not a very nice room, is it? Who would want to come here if they didn't have to?"

Jake and his family kept their mouths shut.

The warden pointed at the crumbs and blobs of cheese sauce on the table in front of Jake. "I do like to see an enthusiastic eater," she said. "I don't suppose you use placemats in your own home, but I find they're useful for cleanups and give a sense of occasion, even to an ordinary day."

Jake wanted her to shut up, but she kept on talking, chewing up their time.

"Some wardens have made their visiting rooms happy places, with bright colors, comfortable chairs, and toys to play with. I think that just encourages children to turn to a criminal lifestyle, don't you? Enough children of prisoners turn to crime as it is."

She put her hand on Jake's shoulder. Jakeman
pushed the barbed wire up through his skin—pointed
and painful, the best defense ever. Out of the corner of
his eye, Jake saw Harlan step away from the table
where he'd been sitting with his aunt and head in their
direction. Jake didn't move.

"You, young man with the creative eating habits,"
said the warden. "Do you want to spend your life
behind bars, now that you've seen my ugly visiting
room?"

"No," Jake said, adding, after a kick from
Shoshona, "ma'am."

"Then my décor choice has helped you, and for that
I am glad. We can find lessons and blessings in so many
things, if we open our minds to them."

Warden Scofield turned to go, but came face-to-face
with Harlan. Harlan didn't say a word. He just held up
the photo of his mother.

Warden Scofield was not easily intimidated. She
deftly stepped around Harlan, only to be blocked by
Harlan's aunt. She walked a bit more, but was stopped
again, this time by Gitana and her grandmother. They
didn't say anything. They just stood there.

The warden nodded at one of the guards. It was a

very small gesture, but Jake saw it. Then she walked quickly out of the visiting room. No one else got in her way.

The guards moved in. Harlan's aunt and Gitana's grandmother were taken back into the prison. Guards moved in on Harlan and Gitana, too, but Ms. Granite was right there.

"Keep your hands off them," she told the guards. "They can leave on their own. Janice, go with them."

The guards kept their hands away, and Harlan kept his temper. Ms. Granite walked with them to the door, then spoke to Lydia before sitting back down on her bench.

"The girls have a song they'd like to sing for you," Ms. Granite announced.

Lydia got the other two feather-boa girls up and they put on a little show they'd rehearsed at the community center. The moms and kids turned their chairs around to watch.

After the girls sang a couple of Pointer Sisters songs, little Sophie got up and stumbled her way through a lame, little-kid knock-knock joke. Dayton's mom pushed him to his feet. He recited "Casey at the Bat" with lots of expression and hand gestures. Jake had heard him do it before, at a school assembly. He was pretty good.

Then, without prompting, Shoshona got up and sang a song Jake had heard her sing in church. It was about how if she had wings like a dove, she would fly far, far away. It was a good song to sing in a prison.

Time went by quickly after that. Shoshona asked Mom to at least call her lawyer, and Mom said she might, if she could find the phone number, but it was really hard to get to the phones. Then Mom started crying again.

The five-minute buzzer sounded. Jake and Shoshona started to gather themselves up.

In the old days, when Jake first started coming to the prison, they had all clung to each other until the last possible second. Now they knew better. A quick good-bye was easiest, like yanking an old bandage off an arm.

Jake and Shoshona stood tearless amid the crying Pointer Sisters girls, Dayton and his sister, and even grown-ups, who wailed as loudly as the children. Little Sophie had to be pulled away screaming.

And then all the moms were back behind the prison

door. And Jake and the others were back outside the prison walls.

Dear Mr. Governor,

I saw you on the TV again, giving an award to some-
body. I would like you to give an award to our bus driver,
Mr. Michaels. He drives the bus that brings us to prison to
visit our mother (Shanice Kiera DeShawn, pardon her,
please). He always remembers our names if we're old-
timers, like me and Shoshona. And he greets the new ones
like they are doing him a favor by riding on his bus. He
asks about what we like and don't like, and says we should
all think about becoming bus drivers because we could
drive all over the country and earn good money for college
or whatever else we want to do. He tells us about gears and
traffic signs, and stuff I don't remember. He's always wait-
ing when we get out of the prison, with big boxes of donuts
he lets us have for free! We don't have to pay! He says we
give him the pleasure of our company, so he wants to give
us something in return. And then, real fast, we're back on
the road, eating chocolate or jam donuts. So, please, give
him an award, and pardon my mother. If two things are too

much, just pardon my mother. We'll find our own way to give Mr. Michaels an award.

Respectfully yours,

Jacob Tyronne DeShawn

CHAPTER 7

Outside, it was all wailing and weeping.

Jake leaned against the prison wall with the other old-timers and watched Ms. Granite, Janice, and Shoshona look after the weepers. The tall man with the long dreadlocks carried away the crying Sophie. All Jake could see of her was her head full of hair ribbons.

Mr. Nothing and the bus were nowhere in sight.

"Gitana, run around the corner. See if the bus is in the parking lot," Ms. Granite said.

"I'll go with her," Jake offered, and left before anyone could stop him.

The bus wasn't there.

"Why did you stand up like that?" Jake asked her.

"You got thrown out."

"We were standing with Harlan," Gitana told him in a voice that said she thought he was an idiot for asking.

"With Harlan? Why? He's mean."

"He's angry. He's not mean. Aren't you angry?"

"I'm angry that Harlan is mean to me." They started walking slowly back to the others. There was no reason to hurry, and Jake liked walking with her.

"We have to stick together," Gitana said. "My grandmother taught me that."

"What's she in for?"

"Sedition."

Jake had never heard that word. He didn't want to show his ignorance, but he had to ask. "What's sedition?"

"It means she worked for Puerto Rican independence. She was against the American government in Puerto Rico."

Jake was even more puzzled. "You can go to prison for that?"

"You can if you're Puerto Rican," Gitana said as they rounded the corner of the prison. "She got ninety-eight years."

Jake stopped walking and let Gitana get ahead of him. Ninety-eight years. He touched the wall of the prison. It was solid and cold.

An hour went by, maybe more. All the crying stopped, to be replaced by dull emptiness and quiet misery. Jake pressed himself against the wall, thinking of his mother on the other side, unable to get out.

Jakeman could smash the walls, beat up the guards, and melt the barbed wire with his bare hands. Jake tried to imagine how great that would feel, and how shocked the guards would look. But that lasted for only a little while. That was the problem with getting older—daydreams didn't last as long as they used to. He was plain old Jake, leaning against that hard, high wall.

"I forgot this was her sweater," Shoshona said. "I should have remembered, but I forgot."

"Mom wasn't mad," Jake offered, even though he thought she was, a little.

"She didn't used to be like this," Shoshona said. "Do you remember? Rodney was bad news, but even when he was around, she was always...trying. It's not good for her, being in there."

Jake felt the ridges of brick beneath his fingers.

"We have to get her out," Shoshona said. "What if Rodney comes after us? What if he blames us for everything?"

"How could he find out where we are?" Jake asked. "Doesn't social services keep it a secret?"

"He could come into the shop," Shoshona said. "He could come in by accident one day to get a sandwich, and I'd be there, and I'd have to serve him."

"Maybe he wouldn't remember you."

"He'd remember me."

Jake thought for a moment. "Maybe you could quit. Get another job."

"I don't want to do that," Shoshona said. "Employers don't like you to jump from job to job. It makes them think there's something wrong with you."

Jake shifted around on his feet, then asked, "Is it our fault that Mom's in there?"

Shoshona didn't answer. Maybe she didn't know. Maybe she didn't want to think about it.

Harlan had been quiet all this time, hunched over in his old military jacket. He started bumping against the wall, bouncing his body. Little bounces, then bigger and bigger ones. Then he sprang completely off the wall, like he was launched, and started to walk away.

"Are you planning to walk all the way back to New York City?" Gitana called after him.

Ms. Granite called for Harlan to come back, but he ignored her and kept walking.

Then Gitana started walking, too. So did a few other kids. Shoshona stuck her claws into Jake to keep him from going, too.

In the middle of all this, the bus finally pulled up and the driver opened the door. Gitana and the others came running back, but Harlan kept walking.

Right away, Ms. Granite started in on the driver.

"Why are you so late?"

"I slept in! You want me to fall asleep at the wheel?"

"Don't you have an alarm clock?"

On and on they argued, while the kids climbed into the bus. Ms. Granite made the driver stop for Harlan. Harlan stood for ages looking at the open door before he got on. Everyone clapped when he stepped on the bus. Jake didn't know why. Maybe because it was the sort of thing that would make Mr. Nothing angry.

There was another fight to get the driver to stop at the McDonald's again to give everyone a bathroom break. Ms. Granite kept the driver waiting and fuming while she bought all the kids a hot chocolate, "to warm the chill out of you," and let them play in the indoor playground. After he changed his clothes, Jake played, too, even though he was too old. He just needed a few minutes of noise and silliness.

Eventually, with the driver snorting and cursing, everyone got back on the bus and the bus got back on the road. It was late, almost dark.

Jake watched the farms and little towns rolling past his window. He saw kids playing in the yards, and being called inside as the sun went down and the houses' lights came on.

He dozed off, his chin dropping to his chest. When he woke up, it was full-blown night, and they were on the freeway.

Except they weren't moving.

"Where are we?" he asked. "Why aren't we moving?"

No one answered him, so he asked again, in a louder voice, waking up the others.

"Shut up," said the driver.

Jake got to his feet and headed down the aisle. "Is there an accident?"

"Sit down."

"I don't see an accident." All he saw was an endless stretch of car lights, end to end, no one moving.

"Someone put this kid back in his seat," Mr. Nothing yelled.

"Go on, Jake," said Ms. Granite, gently. "It's not safe to stand while the bus is moving."

"But the bus isn't moving."

"Well, sit down anyway."

Jake took his seat, because Ms. Granite had asked in a nice voice. The driver started cursing again. Ms. Granite got on his back about bad language, and he yelled back, "You think these kids haven't heard bad words before? That's all they are, bad words on two legs."

That got Gitana and Shoshona and some of the others involved, too. It went on like that for a while until Harlan, of all people, yelled out, "Shut up!" And everybody did.

Ages and ages went by. Nothing moved and nothing happened except when kids whined and Mr. Nothing turned around and yelled, or leaned out the window and yelled. He got out of the bus to see what was going on. Soon after that, the traffic started inching forward again, and he had to haul himself back on the bus.

The bus stopped and started for another couple of hours, until it finally got to the spot where the state police were making vehicles leave the freeway.

"There's an accident ahead," the trooper said. "Chemical spill."

"I got a busload of brats here," the driver complained. "We'll be way off course."

"Get off the freeway" was all the trooper had to say to that.

The driver cursed some more and followed the long, slow-moving line of cars down the side road. After a while, they picked up speed and they were on their way again.

An hour or so later, the throwing up started.

It started with a couple of the smaller kids—one first, then another. Then it hit the bigger kids. Then even Ms. Granite and Janice threw up. All over the bus, there was moaning and puking and crying.

The driver yelled and steered the reeking bus over to the side of the road. All the sick kids got out to puke some more, and all the non-sick ones got out to escape the stink.

Jake and Shoshona were among the non-sick ones. Shoshona helped the others, of course. Jake leaned against the bus, next to Dayton and Carolyn, who weren't sick either. Together they listened to the others puking and crying.

"Is it always like this?" Dayton asked. He had a firm grip on Carolyn so she wouldn't wander off.

"First time," Jake said.

"We have to get them to a hospital," said Shoshona.

"They can go to the hospital in the city," said the driver. "I'm not making another stop."

"The city is six or seven hours away. These people need medical care now." Some of the kids were doubled over on the ground. "They're real sick," Shoshona said.

"Do you see a hospital? Stop acting like you know more than I do."

While the driver and Shoshona argued, Harlan rooted around in the trash by the driver's seat, found a map, and read it by the bus headlights.

"There's a hospital a few miles away," Harlan said, slamming the map against the driver's stomach.

The driver grabbed for Harlan, but little Ricardo got in the way. The driver tripped and sprawled in the gravel, which did not help his mood. He bullied

91

everyone back into the bus. Harlan stood over him as the bus got back on the road, telling him which way to turn.

The bus drove into a small town and pulled in to the hospital parking lot. Shoshona jumped out first and ran to the emergency room. Soon, nurses and orderlies were helping the sick ones off the bus. The rest of the kids followed them inside.

"My briefcase!" Ms. Granite called out, as she was being carried away on a stretcher. "Leave it with hospital security!"

"We'll take care of it," Gitana yelled after her. Jake noticed she didn't say how.

The non-sick kids filed into the waiting room.

"It sure is a small hospital," said Dayton. "I was in the hospital for my appendix, and it was huge. This is like a toy hospital."

"It's a small town," said Shoshona. "What did you expect?"

"Queen of Pain?" Dayton asked Jake. "You got that right." He walked away. Jake started to follow Dayton.

Shoshona grabbed Jake's collar. "Where do you think you're going?"

"Exploring."

"No, you're not. You're going to help me clean the bus."

"Why should *we* clean it? It's not our bus."

"It's ours if we have to ride in it," Shoshona said. She got buckets and mops and rags and disinfectant from the hospital staff, and they went to work. The bus was parked under some streetlights, so they could see the puddles of puke. It was disgusting work.

"Better to clean it than sit in it," Shoshona said to stop Jake's complaining. He refused to agree with her, even though he knew she was right.

Shoshona left the bus doors open, to air it out, so Jake took his backpack out with him. You never could tell who could be wandering around in small towns, looking for comic book ideas to steal.

After that, there was nothing to do but sit in the waiting room, along with a woman with a black eye and a smashed-up face, a young man holding a whimpering baby, and an old man holding his stomach.

"Stay together," Shoshona ordered. But the only kids who obeyed her were the few who had fallen asleep on seats. Jake grabbed Dayton and they went exploring. They found the driver in the cafeteria, chomping his way through a big plate of chicken.

They were in the middle of a good game of elevator tag when the hospital security staff caught up with them. Jake and Dayton were herded back into the waiting room with the others. A guard was posted by the door to keep an eye on them.

"Carolyn's done it again," Dayton said. His little sister was sitting off by herself.

"What?"

"She's got a cat or something in her jacket."

"How can you tell?"

"Look."

Jake looked. Carolyn had on a pink jacket that buttoned up. Her arms were across her chest, and it looked like she was cuddling something. She also looked happy.

"She used to have a cat she called Sunny. It was an ugly, mean thing," Dayton said. "It liked to leap on people. It jumped on the police when they came to arrest Mom. They shot it, right in front of her. Now everyone says she has problems. Well, duh! Now she steals pets and doesn't talk." He sounded angry. "What do they expect?"

Jake stared at whatever it was squirming inside of

Carolyn's jacket. "Where would she get a cat in a hospital?" he whispered, just as a long white ear stuck up out of the top of her jacket. "Or is that a rabbit?"

"She finds them." Dayton sighed, and got up out of his chair.

Carolyn saw him coming, and crawled under her seat to get away. She squished herself as far from Dayton as she could.

The others joined in for something to do. Carolyn kicked and punched, but they pulled her out. After all, she was only seven, and everyone else was older and bigger.

The security guard grabbed hold of the rabbit by the scruff of its neck. "Where did you get this? Did you steal this from the lab?"

Carolyn looked in another direction and wouldn't answer.

"This is a living thing!" the guard shouted. "It's not a toy!" The guard shoved his big face down by Carolyn's small one.

"You got your rabbit back," Jake said, stepping in between them. "Take it back to its cage before it craps all over the waiting room."

The rabbit took that moment to pee on the guard's

shoe. The guard made angry-guard noises and huffed his way out of the waiting room.

Jake got his back patted and congratulated for his bravery. He tried to do what Jakeman would do—pretend it was no big deal.

He sat back in his seat and got a good look at the kids who still had their guts intact. There was Gitana, still reading her way through the *New York Times* and a couple of other newspapers she'd picked up in the waiting room. Two of the three Pointer Sisters girls, Lydia and Rochelle, were asleep on one sofa. Manuel and Ricardo Hernandez were asleep on another. Jake counted on his fingers—five, plus Dayton, Carolyn, Shoshona, and him. Nine. Nine kids left.

"Is Harlan sick, too?" Jake asked hopefully.

"No, he isn't," Shoshona said. "Go find him."

"Me? No. Why?"

"You want the security guards to grab him?"

"Why not?"

"Use your head. He'll get himself into trouble. Go. Now."

There was no point in arguing with the Queen of Pain. She always won. Besides, wandering was more fun than sitting.

Jake looked all over the small hospital. Harlan had probably gone walking again, but there was no use in going back. It sure beat trying to get Shoshona to believe that he'd really looked everywhere.

He finally found Harlan in the maternity ward.

Harlan was standing at the window where they kept all the new babies. He had his fingertips on the glass, and his face wasn't angry. He looked like he was talking to them in some kind of secret Harlan-to-baby language, from his mind to theirs. There was no one else in the hall.

Jake didn't want to startle him, so he shuffled his feet a bit.

Harlan turned, saw Jake, then jerked his head a bit, inviting Jake to join him and look. Jake didn't want to go anywhere near Harlan. But he didn't want to say no, either. He went over to the window.

There were four babies in the nursery, all wrinkled and sleeping and tiny. They wore wool hats like it was winter, and slept in tiny doll beds.

"We used to be like them," Harlan said.

It was hard to imagine.

"And one day, they'll be like us," Jake said.

"Yeah," said Harlan. "Too bad, isn't it?"

Jake didn't know how to answer that, so he just said, "We're all supposed to be in the waiting room." To his shock, Harlan actually turned and walked back down the corridor with him. They didn't talk on the way down.

Back in the waiting room, all the kids were awake. Mr. Nothing was there also, sitting as far away from the group as he could. He was looking over the map. Then he got tired of that and tossed it on the table. The map missed and fell to the floor.

"Give me a part of your newspaper," he said to Gitana.

Gitana responded by moving the papers out of his reach.

Jake laughed and sat by Dayton. He opened his backpack and took out his art book, even though it wasn't an Old Masters type of drawing he was going to do. With a regular school pen, he drew Mr. Nothing, bigger and puffier than he actually was, looking all grumpy and uncomfortable on too-small furniture.

"That's good," Rochelle said, looking over his shoulder. "What else can you draw?"

"Show her Jakeman," Dayton said. "Jake draws great comics."

Jake wasn't sure he was ready to show Jakeman to all these people, but he reached into his backpack anyway. Maybe they'd say more kind things.

A doctor strode into the waiting room and looked around. "Who's in charge of this group now?" she asked.

"I suppose I am," the driver said, looking like every word he spoke tasted bad.

The doctor handed him a piece of paper. "Ms. Granite asked me to give you this. It's the phone number of her office in New York. If you call in the morning, they'll send another couple of workers up here to help get the kids back to the city."

"You mean I have to stay here all night? With them?"

"We could try to find emergency foster homes for them for the night, but we're a small community. We don't have the resources to deal with a big group all at once. You can all sleep here in the waiting room. It's safe."

"Can't I just drive them back now?"

"Ms. Granite just suggested you call this number, that you might not be equipped to handle the special needs—"

"They're a bunch of wackos and criminals," he growled. "But I think I can handle 'em."

"How is Ms. Granite?" Shoshona asked. "How are all of them?"

"We'll need to keep them for a day or two at least. Perhaps longer. They're very sick. It looks like food poisoning, which can be serious, but we're taking good care of them. Now, if you'll excuse me." She went back to work.

"This is a nightmare," said Mr. Nothing. "This is the worse night of my life, stuck here with sick people and juvenile delinquents."

"Don't forget *yourself*," Gitana said from behind her newspaper. "You're stuck with yourself, too. That's worse than anything."

Mr. Nothing snapped. He jumped up. "That's it! I'm not waiting. I'm not putting myself out for the likes of you. I'm driving back tonight." He stomped out of the waiting room.

Without even hesitating or discussing it, Jake and all the others got up and followed him out. Mr. Nothing tried to close the bus door on them, but Harlan pushed it open and held it that way until everyone got on.

"Drive carefully," Harlan said, just before sitting down.

Curses flew, the bus started up, and they drove away from the hospital.

Jake couldn't smell the sick smell anymore. All he could smell was disinfectant. Shoshona was a good cleaner. She was turning him into one, too, whether he liked it or not.

Dear Mr. Governor,

I hope you had a good Christmas. This was our first Christmas without Mom. We had a visit with her, and we sang some carols. There was a cake, too, with Happy Holidays on it, but that warden butted in and took all the fun away. We brought in a parcel for Mom, but it was just the regular, like socks and coffee. We couldn't get her anything special. She couldn't get us anything at all.

On Christmas Day, Shoshona sang a solo in church, then took me to see the big Christmas tree in Rockefeller Center. We bought hot chocolate and looked at the tree, like we used to do with Mom. We were in trouble when we got back to the foster home. Shoshona doesn't believe in asking permission.

It's New Year's Eve soon, and I hope you have fun. If you're looking for a New Year's resolution, I have one for you, and I bet you can guess what it is!

Happy New Year.

Respectfully yours,

Jacob Tyronne DeShawn

It was like being in a classroom without a teacher, a group home without house parents, detention without a supervisor. With Ms. Granite and Janice gone, the bus was on recess.

Harlan kept quiet and Carolyn said nothing, of course. And Shoshona behaved, but she couldn't stop Jake and the others bouncing around and breathing in the freedom. It was almost an adventure.

"All of you, shut up!" the driver yelled. "Sit in your seats with your mouths closed or I'll dump you all in a ditch!"

Everyone settled down pretty fast, not because Mr. Nothing told them to, but because it was late, and they were all tired. Still, not more than a minute passed before the quiet was broken by little Ricardo singing, "The wheels on the bus go round and round."

They sang a couple of verses. The driver pretended not to hear, even when they changed the words. "The belt on the driver goes round and round," and "The pants on the driver go on and on." It didn't last long.

Jake made himself as comfortable as he could and watched the world go by the window as he waited for sleep. They drove through a little town, hardly even big enough to be a town. It had a Waffle House. The light on the W was out. It said Affle House.

Affle House. That's funny, thought Jake, and he drifted off to sleep.

He opened his eyes after a while to see that same Affle House sign again. Or at least it was another one just like it.

"Are we lost?" he said out loud. No one answered him. Everyone was asleep. He got up, went to Shoshona's seat, and gave her arm a shake.

"Wake up. I think we're lost."

Shoshona started to be mad. But then she got mad at the driver instead. She stomped up to the front of the bus.

"Are you sure you know where we're going? Do you want me to check the map for you?"

"Get back in your seat."

"My little brother thinks we're going around in a circle."

"Don't start with me."

"Do you know where we are? Where's the map?"

Gitana spoke up. "You had it in the hospital. Did you leave it there?"

"Sit down!"

All the arguing woke up the others.

"Are we lost?" Manuel asked.

"When are we getting home?" Rochelle called. "We've been driving for ages."

Shoshona rooted around in the mess around the driver's seat.

"Get away!" the driver yelled.

"I'm hoping to find the map. How could you leave it at the hospital?" Shoshona stood up suddenly. "Do I smell booze? Have you been drinking up here? I do smell booze!"

"What I do, prison brat, is none of your business. Now sit down!"

Shoshona wasn't the only one up front now. Jake

was there, and all the others. The driver also started looking for something but Shoshona found it first—an open bottle of whiskey in his jacket pocket.

"You can't drink and drive!"

They'd all seen people drunk. People who couldn't walk straight couldn't drive straight.

Mr. Nothing made a swipe for the bottle and missed. "I'm not drunk," he grunted. "It's just to steady my nerves. They need steadying, after having to put up with all of you."

"That's just what my father says," said Rochelle. "And then he starts swinging."

"Or falling down," Dayton said. "Mine fell down."

"The driver can't fall down," Manuel added helpfully. "He's already sitting down."

"Do you know about Alcoholics Anonymous, driver?" Rochelle asked. "There's Alateen for your kids, too. Do you have kids?"

All the kids had an opinion, and they were all shouting at once.

"We're going to tell the cops on you. You're going to jail."

"And we won't come to visit you, either."

"Enough! Shut up!" Mr. Nothing flung his hand

back, trying to push everyone away from him, but the kids were on a roll.

Then he started spitting out bad things about their mothers.

Carolyn hit him first. It was no little girl slap, either. She put all her seven-year-old mad behind it.

"Hey!" the driver squawked. "Cut that out." He tried to smack her away, but she ducked.

It would have been sensible to leave him alone. It would have been sensible to not throw things, to not yell things, to not crowd around the seat, getting in his face and blocking his view. It would have been sensible. But it had been a long day.

Mr. Nothing roared like a man attacked by killer bees or fire ants or a pack of rabid squirrels. He managed to steer the bus over to the side of the road and stop it while flailing his arms at whoever was closest.

"I've had it! I've had it!" he kept yelling. He thundered to his feet, shaking off the smaller kids. "Out of my way, stupid," he barked at Harlan, giving him a mighty shove and sending him tumbling into the smaller kids.

"Drive yourselves!" he roared. "I'll find my own way home. Monsters! You're monsters!"

He turned and stormed down the stairs.

But, in his anger, Mr. Nothing forgot to duck. The knock to his head could be heard all over the bus.

He staggered. He wavered. He moaned.

He made it out the door. They heard the gravel crunch under his heavy footsteps. Then they heard a *thud* as the earth quivered under the driver's heavy body.

The kids crept off the bus.

Mr. Nothing was a big lump on the grass by the side of the road.

"Is he dead?" Jake asked.

"He looks dead," said Manuel.

"We have to see if he's all right," said Shoshona. She looked to Harlan, who was bigger. But he leaned against the bus, not moving.

Jake thought briefly about checking the driver. But not even Jakeman was that brave.

"I'll check," said Gitana. "I'm faster than him, even if he is bigger."

Shoshona went with her. Jake stood with the others and watched the two girls step closer and closer to the giant lump.

"Hello? Driver? Are you all right?" Gitana picked

up a bit of gravel and tossed it at him gently.

He didn't move.

Jake inched forward with the other kids. Shoshona and Gitana kicked at his feet, then backed away quickly. Still no movement.

In a final, bold step, the girls knelt down beside the mountain of man, gave him a shake, and checked to see if he was breathing.

"He's alive," Shoshona said. "He's just unconscious."

Jake and the others went over to him. He was lying face up in the weeds, his giant belly in the air.

"Help me get him back on the bus," Shoshona said.

The others protested at once.

"*What?*"

"Why?"

"Leave him in the dirt," Harlan said. "That's what he'd do to us."

"So? We're better than he is."

"Better, but not stronger," said Lydia.

"If we all work together, we can do it." Still no one moved. Shoshona threw up her hands in frustration.

"Maybe you haven't noticed that we're still a long way from home."

That got Jake and the others moving. Bits of the driver got lifted—an arm, a leg—but the rest of him stayed firmly on the ground.

"Now what?" asked Dayton.

"Now we cover him with a blanket or something, and wait until he wakes up." No one moved, so Shoshona ordered Jake to get a blanket.

There were a couple of blankets folded up under the back seats. Jake grabbed one and took it out to Shoshona. She spread it out over the lump in the grass.

"At least he left us this," Harlan said, holding up the bottle of booze and jiggling it.

Shoshona started bossing him to throw it away, arguing that it was the last thing they needed. But it was Rochelle who reached right up and took it from him. Harlan tried to snatch it back, but she was too fast. Gitana helped Shoshona keep him away while Rochelle poured the booze out, all over the bus driver's face. She heaved the empty bottle away into the darkness. Then she turned and stared at Harlan with defiance.

"What a waste," Harlan said. He climbed back onto the bus.

"How long do we wait for him to get up?" Jake

asked.

"How would I know?" Shoshona replied.

"I wasn't just asking you," he said. "I was asking everybody. I know you don't know."

"Maybe he's got brain damage," Gitana said. "Some people get hit in the head, they don't recover. My grandmother used to be in demonstrations. She said the police would crack heads and some people would never be the same."

"You mean he might not be able to drive even if he does wake up?" Dayton asked. "What will we do?"

"We could tie him to the back of the bus and drag him along the highway," Jake said. His brilliant suggestion was lost in the noise of the bus starting up and shifting into gear.

The bus started to move, slowly.

"Come on!" someone yelled.

Up the steps everybody ran, until it was just Jake and Shoshona left.

"I'm not staying," Jake yelled. Luckily, his sister wasn't, either. They both jumped on, leaving Mr. Nothing behind, just as the bus picked up speed.

Harlan drove fast, right down the center of the road. There were no other cars on the two-lane highway, and he took full advantage. Shoshona was scream-ing at him to slow down, but he wasn't paying any attention, so she screamed at everyone else to sit down.

"Look out!"

The bus headlights picked up a deer about to cross the road. Harlan slammed on the brakes. Everyone screamed, and the brakes squealed, but the bus stopped and the deer didn't seem to notice.

Jake and the others crowded up front and watched in silence as a whole family of deer, even some babies, came out of the trees on one side of the road and went into the trees on the other side. They walked nice and easy, dainty and perfect.

"Wouldn't it be great to live right out here, without a fence or anything?" said Dayton.

"Sure, until...*bam!*" Harlan made rifle noises.

"Move," Shoshona told Harlan. "We have to go back for the driver, and I'm driving."

"*I'm* driving," said Harlan.

"I'm sixteen," said Shoshona. "I've got a learner's permit and six weeks of driver's ed. How much trouble do you want to be in?"

Jake could have told Harlan not to waste his breath. The Queen of Pain always won.

Harlan glared for a while, but gave up the driver's seat. "You think you can turn this bus around on a two-lane highway without ending up in a ditch? Be my guest."

Shoshona sat down behind the wheel. "I'll just keep turning right," she said. "That should get us back to where the driver is." Harlan tried to show her where to shift gears but she waved him off.

"Mr. Michaels showed us both," said Jake.

"Shut up," Harlan snarled. Jake did.

Shoshona had a slow, bumpy start as she got used to the bus. A car came up behind them and honked in protest.

"Jake, come up and help me," she said. He stood at the front beside her and looked for right-hand turns.

They kept turning, but the roads kept getting smaller.

"You're doing a lousy job," she told Jake.

"Don't blame me for the roads," he said. "You hate not being right."

The next road they turned onto was all gravel, and the one after that was dirt.

Jake pointed. "There's another one."

Shoshona turned right again, but then the road gave out.

113

"It's gone," she said. She stopped the bus.

Everyone gathered up front. The headlights showed grass and bushes, but no road.

"That's that," she said. She turned off the engine, and she turned off the lights. The bus and the children were plunged into darkness.

It never got dark in the city. Not completely. There were store lights, and car lights, and streetlights. And if there were spots where the lights didn't reach, people learned pretty fast to stay away from them.

The kids didn't know what to do with the darkness. Some begged for the lights. Some started to cry.

"The dead bus driver's out there!" Jake whispered loudly. "He's coming for us!"

Shoshona gave Jake a swat. How did she know it was him? He'd disguised his voice. He wondered how her hand managed to find his head in the pitch dark.

Everyone groped their way to a seat. Jake accidentally sat beside Gitana. She pushed him away.

"I can't turn the lights back on," Shoshona said. "The battery will wear down and we'll be stuck here forever. We'll stay put until it gets light out. Then we'll figure out what to do."

"You mean, stay here all night?" asked Dayton.

"Wouldn't it be great to live like the deer?" teased Jake, although he felt sorry right after.

For a long while, things didn't go so well. No one liked the dark. Some blamed Harlan, some blamed Shoshona. Others threw insults and and hit out at anyone they could reach. Even the Pointer Sisters girls got into a big fight. It looked like everyone would end up angry and fighting.

Then Ricardo announced that he had to go to the bathroom.

"Me, too," said Lydia.

Everybody did.

"What do we do?" Manuel sounded anxious.

Nobody wanted to leave the bus. It was too dark outside. It was dark inside the bus, too, but at least they were all together—even if they were fighting. The walls made them feel protected. Whatever was out there couldn't get them if they stayed inside.

"This is silly," said Shoshona. "Harlan, you and I are the oldest. We have to look after the little ones."

"Who are you calling little?" Jake demanded.

"You, pea-brain, if you don't stop acting like an idiot. We'll go out in groups. Girls first, then boys. And no peeking."

The boys started to brag that they had no reason to peek, they'd seen everything before. Shoshona got all the girls together and did a count-off. Five girls, including Carolyn, who didn't talk. They went off into the dark, giggling, and the boys made wolf noises to try to scare them.

Then it was the boys' turn.

Jake stumbled off the bus. He was scared. He'd never been in that much dark before. But then he saw that the night wasn't just dark. It was shadows and different shades of dark.

And then he saw the sky.

It took his breath away. All those lights! He'd learned about the solar system in school. His teacher said there were billions of stars, but he had learned a lot of things in school, with no proof that any of it was true. He had to admit, though, his teachers weren't lying about the stars.

The night air felt good, and it smelled good. Everything was quiet. No traffic. No car alarms. No radios. Nobody screaming.

Jake felt like a man, standing tall on the planet, late, late at night.

Everyone was in a better mood when they got back

on the bus, like they'd conquered something.

Jake's eyes were finally adjusted to the night. He found his way to an empty seat behind Shoshona. She helped him get comfortable.

"Sing something," he told her. Then, afraid she'd burst into one of those opera things she was always practicing, he added, "Sing something normal."

Shoshona sang something she hadn't sung since the early days after their mother was taken. She sang it slow and quiet. The words and tune wrapped themselves around the kids, lost in the bus, and gave them comfort in the cold, dark night.

Shoshona sang "America the Beautiful."

She sang it a second time, and because everybody knew it, they joined in. Gitana and the Hernandez brothers sang it in Spanish. Shoshona and Jake remembered the old harmonies. Then the Hernandez brothers sang something from Mexico. Lydia sang an old nursery rhyme. Gitana sang a Puerto Rican folk song. The songs were soft and easy on tired ears.

It went on like that through the night. Everyone had a song their mom used to sing to them at bedtime. Jake moved up to sit with his sister. Kids doubled up in the seats, staying close. They got through the night with whispers and songs.

And when they weren't singing or whispering, they thought about their moms. And they wondered if their moms were thinking about them.

Dear Mr. Governor,

Shoshona cried today. Shoshona never cries, but today she did, and it was in front of a whole church full of people. Do you go to church? Do you have to wear a suit? I bet you have to wear a suit a lot. That must be the worst part about being governor. My suit is ugly, and big, and ugly again. But that's not why Shoshona was crying.

She was singing a solo in church. She does that a lot. She was singing this song, "Sometimes I Feel Like a Motherless Child." I don't know why they made her sing that song. There are happier church songs. She was in the middle of it, and doing fine, but she got to the line, "Motherless children have a real hard time," and she started to cry. I cried, too, all over my suit. The choir covered for her, so it sounded all right, but that's not the point.

The point is, I don't want to see Shoshona crying again. Get our mother out of prison. I've been writing to you and writing to you. What's taking you so long?

I'm beginning to think you don't care. Not about kids, or mothers, or me.

Not so respectfully yours,

Jacob Tyronne DeShawn

The night was pushed away by the day. Jake started to realize he could see trees and fields, not just shapes and shadows. Everything was trapped in mist—hovering, unearthly. He wondered if he could draw that. He wondered if the city ever looked that way.

All over the bus, kids stretched, yawned, and became alert to the day. They'd made it through the night.

"You drove us into the wilderness," Jake said to his sister.

"It's not the wilderness," Shoshona said. "It's the country."

The bus was sitting in a big field, with trees all

around it.

Jake had to go to the bathroom again. It wasn't scary anymore, but now he had to worry about the girls spying on him. He went into the trees with Dayton and the Hernandez brothers, then went off farther by himself.

The birds were waking up and they wanted everyone to know it. They made as much noise as anything the city could come up with. It was a good noise, though. More like music than noise.

He stood off by himself and was feeling fine. Until something butted him in the back.

He jumped and turned around. He was face-to-face with a creature with a giant head.

"A bear! A bear!" Jake shouted, racing back to the bus. He could hear the creature following behind him. "Help!"

Jake burst into the field by the bus. He was met with laughter. Nobody looked worried.

"You're being chased by a cow," Gitana said. "Grow up."

How was he supposed to know? He'd never seen one before. He'd seen pictures, but not the real thing, and certainly not up so close. He hadn't expected the big head.

Carolyn was already hugging the cow. Jake couldn't be scared of something a little girl wasn't afraid of. He stretched out his hand and touched its nose. It was soft and warm.

"Careful it doesn't eat you," Dayton teased.

Everybody laughed. Jake thought briefly about smashing into Dayton to reclaim his dignity, but the sun was coming up and the day was too fine. He fetched his backpack and sat down on a tree stump.

Dayton and Harlan started a game of soccer, kicking a chunk of wood around. Gitana and the Hernandez brothers joined them. Lydia braided Rochelle's hair, and Shoshona walked slowly around the meadow, stretching her back and swinging her arms.

Jake looked at Carolyn, and his art book and good pens came out of his backpack almost before he realized it. "Let the image travel from your eye down your arm to the pen," Rawlins was always saying. "Relax with it. Don't be afraid of it. Let it happen."

The shape of the cow's head came first. Jake turned it slightly, so the cow was looking at Carolyn, and Carolyn was looking at the cow. Jake kept his pen moving, not worrying about what he couldn't do, thinking only about what he could.

"You've made our cow smile," said a voice behind him.

He turned to see a white boy and girl, around his age, maybe a little bit younger. They were dressed in old-fashioned clothes. The boy wore suspenders, and tufts of his blond hair stuck out beneath a wide-brimmed black hat. The girl had on a long dress and wore an apron over it. Her hair hung down in two long braids.

"Our cow. You made her smile," the girl said again, pointing at the drawing.

Jake looked, almost surprised at what he saw. The cow looked as happy to be with Carolyn as Carolyn looked to be with the cow. *Incandescent*, Jake thought.

The other kids saw the strangers and came running over. Gitana was the first to speak.

"Hello," she said, holding out her hand. "I'm Gitana."

"I'm Elijah," the boy said.

"I'm Melinda," the girl said. "We came looking for our cow. She likes to wander. You're on our land."

"Sorry about that," Shoshona told them. "We got a

little lost last night."

"You look weird," Rochelle said. "Why are you dressed like that?"

"We look normal," Elijah said. "We're Amish. You're dressed funny, though."

The Pointer Sisters girls still wore their feather boas.

"Don't ask why," Jake said, afraid the girls would start singing again.

"Will you come up to the house for breakfast?" Elijah asked. "It's just through the trees and across another field."

"We can't," Shoshona answered before anybody else had a chance. "We have to be going. We're on our way back to New York."

"I can," Lydia said. "I'm hungry."

"None of us can stay," Shoshona said again.

"We're fugitives," Dayton said. "On the run."

It didn't take much to get the bus kids to act up, telling tales of bravery and mayhem and trying to act tough.

Jake was adding his two cents' worth when he saw the brother and sister whisper to each other. Then they ran away across the field and into the trees.

"Get on the bus," Shoshona said. "They may be

going for the police. We'd better get out of here."

Dayton had to peel Carolyn off the cow. "She'd bring it on the bus if we let her," he said.

Harlan got into the driver's seat before Shoshona did, and by the time she had badgered him out of it and got the bus started, the two Amish kids were running back toward them across the field. They were each carrying something.

Shoshona opened the door of the bus. Elijah and Melinda ran up the steps.

"Here's some breakfast," Melinda said. "You can take it with you."

They handed Harlan a loaf of bread—real bread, still warm, not in a store bag. They also gave him a jar of homemade strawberry jam.

They were all a little stunned. It was like Mr. Michaels giving them donuts.

"Are you really going to New York City?" Elijah asked.

"We sure are."

"Will you send us a postcard? We collect postcards."

"Jake, get your notebook," Shoshona ordered.

Jake wasn't sure which notebook Shoshona meant.

He grabbed the one with the Jakeman drawings, and a pen. He handed them to Shoshona, and she handed them to Melinda. "Write down your name and address," she told them. "We'll send you plenty of postcards."

"You won't forget?"

"We won't forget."

Elijah and Melinda put their address on a blank page of the notebook, then stepped down from the bus and waved good-bye. Jake tried to get the notebook back, but it was intercepted by Rochelle. She and Lydia started looking through it. Shoshona drove in a wide circle around the field, avoiding the cow, and got the bus back onto the lane that led to the dirt road.

Jake didn't pay much attention to where they were going. He was too busy watching his notebook full of Jakeman drawings being pawed over. Dayton knew about Jakeman, but only a little bit—only what the teacher displayed in class as an example of what not to do during a math test. Beyond that, he knew what little bits Jake chose to tell him. But he didn't know it all. Not even Shoshona had seen his notebooks. She knew he had them, but she'd never asked what was in them.

Harlan tore hunks of bread from the warm loaf.

Jake got his, dipped it in the strawberry jam that actually tasted like strawberries, and sat back, watching his notebook. Kids were careful not to drop jam on it.

Shoshona told everyone to get in their seats, but they ignored her. They were too busy looking at Jakeman.

"Did you draw this?" Rochelle asked.

"If you don't like it, give it back," Jake said defensively.

"It's great," said Lydia.

"Put me in it," said Manuel. "And Ricardo. We could be superheroes, too."

"I told you to sit down while the bus is on the road," Shoshona said. "What are you looking at?"

"Jake's comic book," said Dayton.

"Oh. That."

Jake didn't want to hear it. He had told Shoshona once that he wanted to be a comic-book artist, and she shot him down. "Art is a hobby," she'd said. "Spend your time on schoolwork. How are you going to pay your rent when you get older? You need to be realistic."

Like her singing on the stage at Lincoln Center was really going to happen.

He grabbed the notebook out of Dayton's hand and stuffed it in his backpack. "You heard my sister. Sit down." He went to sit at the very back of the bus, far away from everyone, and kept his face to the window.

The others took their seats and left him alone.

"Are we going home now?" Lydia asked.

"I'm going back for the driver," said Shoshona.

"He won't still be there," said Harlan. "We don't need him. You can drive and I can drive."

"Yeah, you're a *great* driver," said Gitana, but not meaning it.

"Better than you," said Harlan.

"I'm just thirteen, so that's not much of an accomplishment. Even if we find the driver, he's not going to want to take us anywhere."

"Sure he will," said Shoshona. "He'll lose his job if we show up in the city without him. He takes us home, we keep our mouths shut about the drinking, and he keeps his mouth shut about us."

"First you have to find him," said Harlan. "You're not going to do that."

"*We,*" said Shoshona. "We're in this together, unless you want to get out."

"Just open the doors," Harlan said. Shoshona

didn't, and he didn't press her to.

It was Carolyn who finally spotted the blanket, hitting her brother on the head to draw attention to it in the grass. Shoshona brought the bus to an uneasy stop and they all got out and ran back.

The blanket, still stinking of booze, was in a heap, without the driver.

"Maybe Martians came and beamed him into space," Ricardo suggested.

"You think the Martians would want him?" Lydia asked.

"At least we know he walked away," said Shoshona. "He couldn't have been hurt badly if he walked away."

"Can we go now?" asked Harlan.

"What's your hurry? You got some fabulous life back in the city you want to get back to?" Gitana asked. She didn't wait for an answer but started walking through the long grass and weeds.

"Where are you going?" Jake called after her.

"He made a trail," she said.

They all filed after her. The trail went through garbage-strewn weeds and lame-looking trees, and came out behind a farm. The barn, the house, the trees, all leaned lazily to one side. They looked like a tornado had hit them.

"Where is everybody?" asked Rochelle.

"Still asleep," said Lydia. "It's Sunday. They're sleeping in."

Rochelle said, "Let's sing them awake."

"Keep quiet!" Shoshona told them. "We should go back to the bus. The driver's okay, so let's just go." But she kept following along.

"Your sister's a bit of a tyrant, isn't she?" Gitana asked Jake.

"She's the Queen of Pain," he said.

"From the comic book. I remember," said Gitana. Jake felt like flying.

They walked up to a weathered clapboard shed.

"Shhhh!" whispered Gitana. "I hear something."

They all shut up and listened.

"That's snoring," said Rochelle.

They inched up to the window of the shed and peered through the glass. Jake lifted up Ricardo, who was too small to see through the glass on his own.

There was just enough light to see the mountain of Mr. Nothing, spread out on an old sofa, snoring away. He wasn't alone. Jake counted four other men on sofas or in easy chairs, asleep and snoring. Stacks of beer boxes and messes of empty cans filled the rest of the shed.

"Looks like he found some friends," Rochelle said. "Let's scare them and wake them up."

"Let's just go," Shoshona said. "And quietly."

Jake and the others had seen enough. He put Ricardo back on the ground, and they backed away from the window.

That's when they heard the first shot.

They were city kids. They knew the sound of gun-shots, but always before, the gunfire had been accompanied by traffic, alarms, and lots of city noise.

This time, it was a strong, loud noise cracking through the quiet of the country morning. Dogs barked and birds flew. And on the back porch of the farm-house, a woman in a nightgown held up a shotgun and screamed, "Thieves! Burglars! Trespassers!"

She fired another shot into the air.

The children ran. Back through the broken-down farm, back down the grass-and-garbage trail.

"Are we all here?" Shoshona panted. "Quick, count—is everybody here?"

Everybody was. Shoshona started the bus, and they

got back on the road.

"At least we don't have to worry about the driver," she said, when she had caught her breath.

"Did he know those guys, do you think?"

"Doesn't matter," said Rochelle. "Drinkers always find drinkers. There were always people passed out and snoring at my house."

"He's not our problem," Gitana said. "We should figure out where we are, and then head for home."

"There's something else," Shoshona said. "By now we'll be missed. Ms. Granite's probably phoned her office, and people will know we're not where we're supposed to be. But we still might get out of this without trouble. They'll get their bus back, and maybe that's all they'll care about. But we've got to have gas, and that means money. Everybody, empty your pockets."

Nobody wanted to part with money, even if it was for their own good. Nobody had much, and they wanted to hold on to it.

"I'll collect," said Gitana. "Come on, everybody. Time to share."

She was ruthless. It came out of reluctant pockets in nickels and dimes, quarters, and crumpled dollars.

"Just over twenty dollars," Gitana said, counting it

up. "How far will that get us?"

"We'll need food, too," said Rochelle. "It's a long trip."

"We can eat when we get home," Shoshona said.

"No one's getting home on twenty dollars of gas," Harlan said. "We're going to have to hitchhike, or steal. Or maybe knock off a gas station or something."

That set Shoshona and Harlan off on a big argument. Jake enjoyed it for a while, but then it got a little too heated to be fun to watch. It even got a little scary. Harlan and Shoshona were the closest things to grownups on the bus. If they didn't know what to do, how would anybody?

Instead of telling the two of them to shut up, Jake and the others started in on each other, sniping and whining. The two Pointer Sisters girls got into a big fight over who could sing better, swore they'd never talk to each other again, and found separate seats.

"Everybody shut up!" roared Gitana. "Shut up and watch for a gas station."

Everybody shut up and kept their eyes open.

There were more cars on the road now. Shoshona drove very slowly and cautiously. Sometimes there was a line of cars behind them, waiting to pass. Some of the

drivers honked and made rude gestures as they drove
by. The kids on the bus gave the insults right back.

"I see a gas station," Jake called out. "Just ahead,
on the right."

The gas station was old and small, with a diner
inside, peeling paint, and a yard full of rusty car parts.
There wasn't much else at the intersection, except a
boarded-up motel across the highway and a few run
down houses. A big, ugly yellow dog with a chewed-up
ear strained at his rope, barking.

Shoshona managed to steer the bus alongside the
gas pumps. "Does anybody know how to do this?" she
asked. "The driver's-ed car always has gas in it
already."

"Turn off the motor," Harlan said. "Don't you even
know that?"

They started an argument about where the gas tank
was and how to open it, but they didn't get very far.

"Someone's coming," said Ricardo.

The door of the little gas station opened. A middle-
aged man came out, Sunday-morning stubble still on
his face.

"I'll do the talking," Shoshona said. "All of you,
keep quiet and stay inside." She collected the money

135

from Gitana and stepped off the bus. Naturally, everyone ignored her and got out, too.

The gas station owner yelled at the dog to shut up. He took a long look at the line of crumpled kids leaning against the bus, and asked, "You the Partridge family?"

"We just need some gas," Shoshona said. "Twenty dollars' worth, please."

"Big spenders," the man said, heading to the pump.

There wasn't much to see outside, so Jake headed into the diner with Dayton. They had no money to spend, but it was something to do.

"Restrooms are for customers only," the woman behind the counter was telling Gitana and the Pointer Sisters girls. She poured coffee for a couple of men who were shoveling pie into their faces. "Hey! Are you gonna *buy* that magazine?"

Harlan was standing by the magazine rack, leafing through a motorcycle magazine. He had his back to her.

"You wanna look, you gotta pay," the woman said, coming out from behind the counter. "This is a store, not a library. I don't need no filthy fingers all over the merchandise."

She went right up into Harlan's space. Jake was

afraid he would hit her, and that would mean real trouble. But all he did was drop the magazine on the floor before leaving the shop. The diner woman picked up the undamaged magazine, dusted it off, and put it back on the rack. She went back behind the counter.

"I hate them Mohawks," one of the men said. He was eating blueberry pie and had a dribble of blue spit on his chin.

"I hate them Mexicans," his friend said.

"And we both hate..." They didn't say what they both hated, but they looked hard at Jake and the other black kids.

"Americans?" Gitana finished for them.

"All right," said the woman. "If you're not gonna buy anything, get on your way. I'm not running no nursery."

"We need a map," Gitana said.

"You out on the road without a map?" Blue-Spit Man asked. "Don'tcha know where you're going?"

"We know where we're going," Jake said. "We just don't know how to get there." He spied a rack of maps beside the magazines. He picked one up. "Can we have this?"

"Cost you five bucks," the woman said.

Gitana took the map from Jake. "This is put out by the New York State Tourism Board," she said. "They give these things away for free, and you're trying to charge a bunch of kids for one. Jake, make a note of that. He and the governor are pen pals," she added.

"Pen pals? What?" the woman stumbled.

Jake wasn't sure if Gitana meant he should actually make a note—he'd left his backpack on the bus—but he didn't have time to ask. Shoshona gave two quick honks on the bus horn, and the kids ran out.

"Where's Carolyn?" Dayton yelled. "Where's my sister?"

Jake saw her little face at one of the windows. "She's on the bus." He saw Harlan there, too. "We're all here."

Just the same, Shoshona made them count off. Then she started up the bus and moved back out onto the road.

Dear Mr. Governor,

My art teacher used to be in prison.

His name is Rawlins. He spent ten years in Attica, which is a very big prison for men, even bigger than Wickham. He won't tell me what he was in for, except that he was in a gang and doing stupid things, and ignoring what he was meant to do. He means he was meant to do art. That was his real love, but the people around him told him drawing was for children, and men needed to fight, or they were cowards. So he'd go off to a fight and do all the things he was supposed to do in a gang, and ignored what was in his heart.

When he got to Attica, he worked in the sickroom, looking after the old prisoners who were dying. One of them died and left Rawlins his art supplies.

Now he volunteers at the Boys and Girls Club, and teaches me art, and sells lots of paintings.

I'm telling you this because even if you think my mother is a bad person, she isn't. People can change, and you should give her a pardon.

Respectfully yours,

Jacob Tyronne DeShawn

What's that smell?" Shoshona asked. She was more comfortable now behind the wheel of the bus and was able to pick up speed a little. She didn't drive Harlan-fast, but cars stopped honking and other drivers stopped making rude hand gestures.

No one answered her.

"There's a terrible smell on the bus," Shoshona said again.

Everyone started to giggle a little, which no one was very good at hiding.

"What's going on?" Shoshona asked. "Somebody talk to me."

At that moment, a big, ugly yellow dog lifted its

head up off Carolyn's lap, gave one good *woof!*, and then put its head back down.

The bus swerved a little as Shoshona jumped and looked behind her. "You stole their dog? We're driving with a stolen dog?"

"He belongs with Carolyn," Dayton said. "He was just living in the wrong place."

"Yeah. He was living in a foster home!" Rochelle said, which made everyone laugh, even Shoshona.

Jake sat across the aisle from Carolyn. The dog did smell bad. He also had sores and bald spots where his fur had been torn away. But he looked completely contented with his big head across Carolyn's legs. Jake smiled. Something was fixed.

"I have to go to the bathroom," said Dayton. "And I'm hungry."

"We're *all* hungry," said Rochelle. "We all probably have to go to the bathroom, too."

"Then you should all look for someplace," said Shoshona. "It's not just my job."

"Nobody said it was," said Harlan.

Shoshona let that pass.

The problem was, they weren't in the country anymore. They couldn't just go into the bushes because there weren't any bushes. There were car dealerships and lots of houses, but no place where ten kids and one dog could go to the bathroom.

"Pull in there, up ahead." Gitana was at the front with Shoshona, looking for bathrooms. "It's a church. They'll have bathrooms. And they'll have to let us use them."

The Faith Temple of Miracles was a big, modern building. It had a huge sign in front, all lit up, welcoming everyone in and saying, Join Us for Mother's Day. The parking lot was full of cars. Shoshona didn't even try to park the bus properly. She just pulled in between the rows of cars and left the motor running.

"Quickly in and quickly out," Shoshona ordered, refusing to open the door until she gave her little speech. "Stay together. We use the bathrooms. We get back on the bus. If we're lucky, we can blend in."

Everyone gave their word so that she'd shut up and let them go.

She opened the door, then added, "Leave the dog on the bus."

Carolyn and the dog did not agree to that last part.

The sun had come out and the morning was warm. The church's doors were wide open. Jake could hear

143

music all the way across the parking lot. There was singing and a band.

The service was already underway. The heads of the congregation were all looking toward the choir, and away from the doors where the children entered.

"The only one blending in here is Lydia," said Gitana. Even with their faces turned, it was easy to see the congregation was mostly white. Not even Lydia really blended in, though. The people in the congregation were dressed up nicely, and Lydia looked like she'd been on a bus for two days. They all did.

The congregation didn't notice. They were too busy singing. They had their arms in the air, and they were belting out words that were projected onto the front of the church with an overhead projector.

A sign with an arrow pointed to restrooms down some stairs. They all headed that way.

Jake smelled coffee. When he was finished in the bathroom, he followed his nose to the kitchen. Tables were set up for a party. A Happy Mother's Day banner hung on the wall. The room was colorful and happy, with flowers and placemats crayoned by the junior Sunday school classes.

And there was food.

Tables groaned under the spread of food. There were salads, cold meats, rolls, pies, and a giant Happy Mother's Day cake with pink and white frosting and giant frosting roses.

Besides the coffee, perking away in a giant urn, there were good smells coming from the three ovens along one of the kitchen walls. Jake could identify turkey and casseroles.

And the kids from the bus were there, too.

They'd followed their noses just as Jake had done, and were now stuffing their hungry selves with whatever they could grab. Carolyn was feeding the dog from a big platter of cold roast beef. He gulped down the meat and wagged his tail like crazy.

Jake didn't see his sister. He moved quickly, getting at the food before she got at them, and getting at the roast beef before the dog got it all.

He was bringing a big spoonful of potato salad to his mouth when Shoshona came out of the restroom, her face all shiny and washed. She was in the middle of her fit when two church ladies, all pink and white like the cake, came down from the service to check that the lunch was ready to serve. *Their* fit made Shoshona's sound like a lullaby.

145

"Don't hurt us!" they screamed. "Don't kill us!" Their hands waved and their eyes grew wide and their pale white skin got even paler and whiter.

"Everybody, back to the bus," Shoshona ordered. She started rounding all the kids up.

The ladies kept screaming, but the congregation above was singing such a great thumping celebration song that no one heard. Carolyn's dog was barking and running around, skidding on the waxed floor. He jumped up on one of the ladies, his big paws on her Sunday dress, and gave her a big kiss on her screaming face.

The ladies turned to go back upstairs. Jake raced to the staircase and blocked them from going farther, holding his arms out straight like he did for the search at the prison. "Please stop screaming," he said, although they didn't seem to hear him. "We're just kids!"

He tried to keep count of all his bus mates, who were slipping by, their hands full of food. He couldn't let the ladies up those steps until all the kids were out.

"Take my purse," one lady said, and they both held out their bags. "Just don't hurt us!"

"I don't want your purse!" Were they crazy? What

did they think he would do with a purse—carry it to school? "We're good kids," he added, talking fast. "We just came in to use the bathroom and we saw all this food, and I'm sorry about the dog, but Carolyn's so happy—"

He didn't have time to finish. Harlan grabbed hold of him, actually lifted him off the floor, and ran up the stairs. They were out in the parking lot and running for the bus when they heard the screaming start up again.

Shoshona was standing by the bus, counting off kids as they scrambled up the steps. Harlan and Jake were the last to arrive. Harlan jumped right into the driver's seat. There was no time to argue him out of it. He shifted into gear and drove them back onto the street.

The Hernandez brothers kept watch out the back window. "No one's following us!" Manuel shouted. "Looks like we got away!"

"Watch your speed," Shoshona said. "You start driving fast, you only attract attention."

"I know what I'm doing!" Harlan insisted, and for a few blocks he drove the speed limit, obeyed all the signs, and let other drivers cut in.

Until, "Cops!" shouted Ricardo and Manuel.

"Hold on!" yelled Harlan.

Jake grabbed tightly to the seat in front of him as Harlan revved up to NASCAR speed. He zipped through traffic, zoomed around corners, ignored stoplights, and drove down the wrong side of the street. He drove like in a movie, making that old Department of Corrections garbage can on wheels do things a bus wasn't meant to do.

They sped down the highway, the police on their tail, lights flashing and sirens going. Half the kids shouted for Harlan to stop. Half shouted for him to go faster.

The bus rounded a bend, and they were out of the cops' sight for a moment.

"In there—now!" shouted Gitana.

Harlan made an impossible turn, then came to a stop.

"Heads down!" he yelled.

Jake scrunched down into his seat. He could hear the sirens come closer, closer, closer…then fade away.

Jake raised himself up. All he saw was orange. Their bus was in the middle of a sea of school buses!

"A school bus depot!" he shouted. "Brilliant! We are brilliant!"

"We?" asked Gitana, but he didn't care. Let her claim the idea. They were all in it together, anyway.

Dear Mr. Governor,

I get a present every birthday. It's in a box, all wrapped up, always the same size, and in it are two pairs of socks, a bag of candy, and a toy, usually one of those balls you can throw in the house and not cause any damage. At first, I didn't know who was giving me these presents. I said thank you to my foster parents, but they keep changing, and the presents stayed the same. Then, when I turned ten, I saw a sticker on the box. It said: Boy, 10, and I knew the present wasn't for me. It was for Boy, 10.

It's nice to get a present. No, it's GREAT to get a present, even one that isn't really mine. But one of these days, it'll be a present for ME, from someone who knows ME.

Respectfully yours,

Jacob Tyronne DeShawn

You drive like a superhero," Jake said, forgetting in his admiration that he used to be afraid of Harlan.

"I know all about cars," Harlan said, with something almost like joy flashing across his face. He brushed his hair back from his forehead. "I can make any engine work."

"You going to be a mechanic?" Manuel asked.

"Designer," Harlan told them. "Design cars and build them. Cars, vans, buses—anything that moves."

"Well, I need to stop moving for a while," Shoshona said. "Let's just stay put. Maybe the police will forget about us or think we left the county. And I need to get calm before driving again." She stared hard at Harlan; her look said she wasn't letting him drive again. Harlan didn't care. He shrugged and slid to the floor.

One by one, Jake and the others moved to the floor, too. It was cleaner now, thanks to the scrubbing. They sat in the aisle, backs against the seats, some facing one way and some facing another, so they could all see each other. They passed around the food they'd taken from the church. They were quiet for a moment, chewing on pie and bean salad.

"If we can get out of here without getting caught, I guess we should get as close to the city as we can on the gas we've got, then call social services to come and get us."

This was Shoshona's idea. It wasn't very exciting, but nobody had anything better. Ricardo suggested driving to the ocean and getting on a ship. Rochelle and Lydia wanted to drive to Las Vegas, where they were sure they would be hired for a big show and earn enough money to fly everyone back to New York City. Gitana said she'd rather fly to Puerto Rico, as long as they were flying places. But these weren't really ideas. They were more like fantasies.

"We'll be admitting we can't do it ourselves," Jake said.

"Well, we can't," his sister snapped. "We can't drive a bus without gas, and we can't get gas without money —and, no, we are not stealing any!" She said that last bit with a big glare for anyone who might want to disagree with her.

"Maybe we could put on a show," Lydia suggested. "People do it in the city. They sing or dance on the sidewalk, and people watch and give them money."

"Up here, they're more likely to lynch us than pay us," Gitana said.

"What's lynch?" Ricardo asked.

"Hang from the nearest tree. But maybe Ms. Granite stashed away some money." Gitana got to her feet and took out the social worker's briefcase from where she'd hidden it beneath blankets and bags. She tried to open the clasp, but the case was locked.

"Hand it over," Harlan said. The case was passed from hand to hand to him. He took a set of nail clippers out of his pocket and, with the nail file, soon had the lock picked and the clasps undone. He turned the briefcase so everyone could see it, then he opened it up. It was full of files. Harlan ran his hands through the pockets on the sides and the lid. He turned up a couple of pens, two paper clips, and a roll of breath mints. "No money." He was about to close the case.

"Let me see," Gitana said.

"You think I'm lying?"

"I want to see the files."

The case was passed back. Gitana took the top file and read off the name. "Sampson, Clarice Ann." She looked over at Rochelle and Lydia. "That's your friend, isn't it?"

"She's back at the hospital," Lydia said.

Gitana set the file aside and read out the next one. "DeShawn, Jacob Tyronne." She looked at Jake. "Is that you?"

Jake nodded.

"These are all our files," Gitana said. She handed them out. Everyone got their own.

"Why would Ms. Granite have our files?" Dayton asked. He looked anxious.

"Probably to update them after our prison visit," Shoshona answered. "She probably thought she could save herself some time by doing them on the trip. Or maybe she was going to show them to that student."

"Janice," said Jake, "with the clipboard. I didn't like her." He couldn't quite believe what he was holding.

"Is it all right if we read them?" Lydia asked. "I was always told I couldn't read mine."

In answer, Gitana got up off the floor, went to a seat by herself, and opened her file. The other kids did the same, leaving space between each other for privacy, like in a school exam.

Jake looked at the closed cardboard folder in his hand. It felt funny to be holding it. He'd heard so much about it over the years, ever since his mother was arrested. People kept talking about it. Social workers always said, "I see from your file," and "This will have to go down in your file." Now he was holding it. There was his name, neat and tidy on a label: DeShawn, Jacob Tyronne.

"They do things backwards in the social services," he whispered.

He wanted to bury himself somewhere. He felt like all the other kids could see through the cardboard folder and read through all the things that had been written about him. It felt like the time he was strip-searched by the guards that day he wore underpants with holes in them.

155

He felt small and ashamed. And horrible.

Jake sat and held his file, and thought about how people had written things about him and put them in the file for other people to read, as though his life was any of their business.

He wasn't sure he wanted to know what was inside.

He looked around the bus, at all the heads bent over the files. Dayton whispered to Carolyn, and Manuel read in a low voice to Ricardo.

If they could be brave, so could he. After all, he was Jakeman, the Barbed Wire Boy, and nothing could touch him.

He opened up his file and, just like all the others, he began to read.

DESHAWN, JACOB TYRONNE, file no. 24396
Present age – 11

Jake's bedwetting finally seems to be under control
after nearly three years. This means he may be able to
stay longer in his new foster home, his sixth since being
taken into care by the social services department. He
still has nightmares, however, and he continues his
practice of crawling into closets at night, or, if he is in
a bedroom without a closet, crawling under the bed.
Our attempts to medicate him for this have been
thoroughly sabotaged by his older sister (*DESHAWN,
SHOSHONA IMANI, file no. 24397*). Due to a scarcity
of spaces, we once had to separate the siblings and place
them in different foster homes, but this was met with
great opposition on the part of his sister, and property
destruction at the hands of Jake. This sort of behavior
should not be rewarded, but they are family, and it is
the policy of this office to keep family together when at
all possible.

Jake's close relationship with his sister is a source of
strength and stability for him, but it could also pose a
problem when she ages out of the system in less than
two years. They will almost certainly be separated at
that point, and we are not sure how well Jake will

adjust to that.

His schoolwork is substandard, perhaps due in part to his having to change schools almost every time he changes foster homes. It is unlikely he will successfully complete high school, and like many boys in his situation, he is at high risk for ending up in the criminal justice system.

Both Jacob and his sister have high dreams for the future—Shoshona wants to be an opera singer and Jake wants to have something to do with art. Given their circumstances and Jake's poor school performance, we would be serving them well to encourage them to lower their expectations. It will spare them disappointment and frustration down the line.

Dear Mr. Governor,

This is how it happened.

They came in the night. We were asleep.

They broke down the door and came in with their guns and their helmets, screaming and breaking stuff.

I thought it was Rodney, so I hid under the bed, but they came after me. I put my face on the floor and shut my eyes, but I could still smell their boots. I could still hear my collection of superheroes hit the floor.

The police threw off my mattress, then they grabbed on to me. They pulled me out from under the bed and they laughed at me for wetting myself. "Where's the cocaine?" they yelled. "Where did they stash it?" I couldn't see their faces through their masks. They were just big hard-heads, yelling and hurting.

They took us out of the apartment and down the stairs. Our neighbors opened their doors and watched, but no one tried to stop them. They put Mom in the back of one police car, and they put Shoshona and me in the other.

I thought they were taking us all to jail. I cried and cried. Shoshona cried and cried.

They put us in a little room in the police station with a blanket to cover our pajamas, and when we couldn't cry anymore, they gave us a social worker, and that's how it all started.

I just thought you'd like to know.

Respectfully yours,

Jacob Tyronne DeShawn

CHAPTER 12

W hat's 'inveterate' mean?" Lydia asked, looking up from her file.

"It means without a spine," Jake answered. "We just did that in science."

"That's *invertebrate*," Shoshona corrected. "*Inveterate* is like a habit, I think."

"They're saying I have a habit of lying," Lydia said. "I'm not. I mean, I lie sometimes, but not all the time. It's not a habit, it's just now and then. They got it wrong."

"Carolyn's file says she's unteachable," Dayton said. "She's teachable. I teach her lots of things. She learns. Why do they write stuff that's not right? We would get in trouble for that."

For a minute there was silence.

Then, all over the bus, the kids began to protest—quietly at first, but quickly gaining in strength as they realized how little of their real lives was found in those files.

And then Harlan started yelling, making horrible, sad, primal sounds—sounds that came from some place deep inside him. He flung his file up in the air. All the papers came drifting down over the bus, just like snow.

Gitana ignored Harlan's roar. She picked up one of the pieces of paper from his file, turned it right side up, and started to read out loud. "'Harlan seems incapable of tenderness or empathy. His anger makes him difficult to be around and impossible to get to know.'"

"Shut up!" Harlan yelled. He grabbed the paper out of Gitana's hands. "You like the sound of that? You like the sound of them trashing all over me? Then you'll love this." He looked down at the report, then read, "'At the core of Harlan's anger is his refusal to believe the official version of his mother's death, that no one knew of her illness until it was too late. We feel it is important to continue to emphasize this version of events, especially since it is clear that prison management is covering up the records of his mother's earlier request for medical intervention.' Do you know what that means? It means that they killed her. But will they ever pay? No! You know who will pay? Me." Reading again, he said, "'We are concerned that his temper could one day provoke a violent incident. It is unlikely there is a future for Harlan outside of prison.'"

He crushed the paper in his hand and slammed his fist into the side of the bus. "You think any of you are different?" he yelled at the other kids. "We're all going to become our files."

"What if they *do* know me?" Rochelle asked. "What if they're right?"

"They're not right!" Lydia protested.

"They're so sure," Shoshona said. "I push back, but they're so sure of themselves."

"We're just a job to them," said Gitana. "Part of their job is to write in our files, so they make up a bunch of stuff and collect their paychecks."

"Well, I'm sick of it," said Shoshona, clenching her fists. "I'm sick of all of it. I hate having my life in a file. I hate that Mom's not the same person anymore. I hate getting moved from foster home to foster home. I'm tired of saving up for gift packages for Mom. I want Mom to buy gifts for me! Everything is backwards and upside down. We keep riding this horrible bus, and nothing ever gets any better!" She slumped back in her seat. She looked defeated.

Jake had never seen his sister look like that. She was the one who always knew what to do.

He got to his feet and went to the front of the bus. Such an important announcement had to be made standing up. "I know what will fix everything, for all of us. I've been writing to the governor. I've been asking him to pardon our mother. He can do it. He has the power. I'll ask him to pardon all your mothers, too. And your aunt and grandmother," he added, for the benefit of Harlan and Gitana.

Shoshona's jaw dropped. "You mean you're still doing that? I thought you gave that up years ago. It's like...writing to Santa Claus!"

Jake burned. He'd felt sorry for his sister. Now he wanted to hit her. Instead, he went to his backpack, took out the notebook full of his letters to the governor, and threw it at her.

"He's going to let Mom out, and then she and I will go live someplace nice, just the two of us. You can stay in foster homes until you're ninety, and we won't care!"

Shoshona kicked the notebook back at him. Gitana stopped it as it went by. She picked it up and started leafing through the pages. "I thought you were just bragging when you told me you wrote to him. You sent all these letters?"

Jake nodded. "I wrote out good copies. The notebook is just for rough."

"He ever answer you? Really?"

"I got one letter back," Jake admitted. "I think it was a mistake, though." He fished an envelope out of his backpack and handed it to her. He'd never shown it to anybody before.

It was in an official Governor of the State of New York envelope. Gitana took out the letter and unfolded it. Everyone crowded around to look at it. Even Shoshona.

It was one of Jake's letters—the one about Shoshona crying in church. On top of the letter, in the white space between the return address and the Dear Mr. Governor part, the governor had written a note, probably to his secretary: *Get this kid off my back. He must be a nutcase.*

Shocked into silence, they all stared at the letter. Then they all looked at Jake.

"You kept writing to him after this?" Harlan asked.
Jake nodded. He was feeling a little silly.

"What's that song?" Rochelle asked. "'Sometimes I
Feel Like a Motherless Child'? I think I know it. Sing a
bit of it."

Jake wasn't sure he wanted Shoshona to do that.
He didn't want her to cry again. But Shoshona sang
just the first part.

> Sometimes I feel like a motherless child,
> Sometimes I feel like a motherless child,
> Sometimes I feel like a motherless child,
> A long ways from home, a long ways from home,
> A long ways from home, a long ways from home.

Rochelle sang along. "I do know it. We sang it at
school. I'll teach it to you," she told Lydia. "It's not
Pointer Sisters, but it's still pretty good."

Jake began to feel low and stupid. Writing to the
governor hadn't given him much hope, but it had given
him more hope than anything else since his mom was
taken. And now he had nothing. The other kids were
right to think he was a fool.

Shoshona put her arm around his shoulders. "Never
mind," she said. "Maybe one day you'll be a famous

comic-book artist. Then you can see the governor and call him a nutcase."

Gitana was studying the newspaper. "Why wait until then?" She bent over the map from the gas station. "Why not do it today?"

"Today?" Jake was stunned.

"His mother is in a nursing home not all that far from here," Gitana said, measuring the distance on the map with her fingers. "The governor will be there."

"How do you know?"

"Where else would he be?" she asked. "It's Mother's Day."

"We can't just drive to the nursing home and talk to the governor," Shoshona said. "We won't be allowed near him. We'll get into trouble. We can't..." Shoshona ran out of reasons.

"Let's take a vote," Gitana said. "After all, we're all on this bus together. Who would like to go ask the governor for a few pardons?"

Jake counted seven hands.

Then Harlan's went up, and there were eight.

As he raised his own hand in the air, something began to tickle at the back of Jake's mind. It felt like hope.

CHAPTER 13

Shoshona took some convincing, but she really wanted to do it. Jake could tell. If she didn't want to do something, nobody and nothing could move her.

"We're filthy," she said. "We can't see the governor looking like this."

"He was a kid once," Dayton said.

"Don't bet on it," said Gitana.

"He was probably grubby once himself, is what I meant," Dayton said.

That wasn't good enough for Shoshona, who sent everyone out exploring for a tap where they could at least wash their hands and faces while she tidied the bus. They found the water hose the bus company used to wash the buses. With soap from the shopping bag, everyone washed themselves. Then they washed the dog, being careful of his wounds. He was patient, and smelled better when they were through. Clarice's feather boa was still on the bus. They wove it around the dog's neck, making him look bright and cared for.

They also found a gas pump used to fuel up the school buses before they went out on their rounds. They filled the tank, and Shoshona left a note promising to send money, so that it wouldn't be stealing.

Dayton and Jake gathered up the files and shoved them back into Ms. Granite's briefcase. They didn't look so powerful now. Just cheap cardboard files. Just words on paper.

Gitana stood at the front of the bus next to Shoshona, read the map, and gave directions. Lydia and Rochelle were singing, but they didn't even annoy Jake.

It was good to have a plan, a real plan—not just a giving-up idea like calling social services for help.

The governor's home town was easy to find. It looked like a town out of a movie. The houses were big, the gardens were groomed, and everyone on the sidewalks looked happy. A long banner stretching across the main street read, Hometown of New York's Governor.

"Like that's something to brag about," said Gitana.

"Maybe they're apologizing," said Lydia.

"People never apologize," said Harlan.

The Sunnycrest Nursing Home was right on the edge of town, set back in a park. Shoshona had to make a sharp right turn into a narrow lane. She had a bit of trouble with it, and other drivers honked and complained.

The lane led to a parking lot, and another lane went back to the road. Shoshona parked the bus so it pointed down the second lane. If they had to, they could make an easy getaway.

As usual, she had to give a little speech before she opened the doors. "We should decide what we're going to say," she said. "If the governor's in there, we want to look like we're serious."

"What do you mean, if he's there?" Manuel asked.

"It's Mother's Day."

"Maybe he took her out some place," Rochelle suggested. "Some folks take their mothers out for lunch on Mother's Day."

"He should apologize for what he wrote to Jake," Gitana said.

"I want the prison to admit what they did," Harlan said. "I want them to admit to my face that they killed my mother."

"All right," said Shoshona. "We've got things to ask for."

"Demand," said Gitana.

"Ask," repeated Shoshona. "We'll start out by asking. Be polite, everybody. Stay together. Or maybe just a few of us should go in. Jake, put your suit on."

Jake wasn't having any of that. He knew how to open the bus door as well as Shoshona. He stepped outside and the others followed. He could hear Shoshona trying to keep the dog back, but the dog won.

"Can we just walk in?" Dayton asked Jake anxiously. "Are they going to search us?"

"Don't you know anything?" Jake asked him back, even though he didn't know either. It was time to bluff, pull out his Jakeman bravery. He led the kids up the lane and into the nursing home.

Through the doors was a curious mixture of smells—cooking, talcum powder, perfume, and bedpans.

Flowers decorated every surface. Sun poured in through
the glassed-in room at the back of the main hall.
Nurses, aides, and visitors bustled back and forth.

"I've never seen this many old people in one place
before," Jake said, his Jakeman bravery slipping away.
He'd got the kids through the door, but now he was
too shy to go farther.

Some of the residents were in wheelchairs, some
on sofas. Others walked with canes or pushed little
carts. Some were watching television, looking down
at their feet, or just sitting, waiting for something to
happen. They all turned to look at the new arrivals.

Gitana was holding the newspaper opened on the
page with the photo of the governor's mother. She
scanned the faces. "She's not out here."

A nurse came hurrying by. She stopped, frowned,
and asked, "Is that dog housebroken?"

"More than we are," said Harlan.

"We're here to see the governor," Jake told her.

"The governor? Of the state? He's not here."

"But his mother's here, isn't she?" Gitana spoke up.
"And it's Mother's Day, isn't it?"

"Yes to both those questions, but no to the governor. He never comes here!" She started to laugh and

walk away. "Oh no! He never comes here!"

It didn't take much for the group to fall apart. Harlan hunched down in his jacket. Shoshona and Gitana started bickering. Everyone else scratched their heads and kicked at the walls. Only Carolyn and the dog looked perfectly happy.

"Are you looking for the governor's mother?" an old woman asked Jake. She was bent low over a walker and smelled like lavender and peppermint. "Are you her grandchildren?"

She asked it so nicely and kindly that Jake answered, "Yes, we are."

"You'll find her right down that hall," she said. "I hope you have a lovely visit."

"Thank you," Jake said, and led the way. He was powerful again.

They hadn't gotten very far when an old man in a bright red sweater shuffled up to them. "I am the governor's mother," he said. "It's very nice to see you all." He held out his hand for them to shake. Jake didn't know what to do.

A woman in a wheelchair came up through the group, using her feet to move herself forward.

"Pay no attention to him," she said. "At breakfast

he thought he was the prime minister of Canada." She took his hand and led him away. Jake and the other kids kept walking.

"Are these my children?" Jake heard a woman ask. "Have my children come to see me?"

All the way down the hall, old people smiled at them—real smiles that reached their eyes.

"They like us," Dayton said. "They even like Carolyn's dog."

It was a good walk, the walk down that hall.

"The woman you want is in there," a nurse told them, nodding toward a closed door. "Just knock. She won't mind."

Jake hesitated.

"Just do it," Shoshona said, "or I will."

Jake knocked.

"Come in," they heard someone say.

Jake opened the door and they went in.

The small room held a single bed, a bureau, two chairs, and a little table. There was a poster on the wall about cleaning up New York's rivers, and another demanding more funding for libraries. A Teacher of the Year award sat on the bureau. A small television set was tuned to an all-day news channel, but the sound was off. An old woman was sitting in one chair. An old man was sitting in the other. They were bent over an open book.

Jake and the others could all see what was going on. They recognized it immediately.

She was teaching him to read.

CHAPTER 14

The kids stayed quiet. They could see the man was struggling, and they knew what that was like. They didn't want to interrupt.

When the old man got to the end of what he was reading, he looked up with relief. The kids all applauded.

"Thank you, children," he said. "That's very kind."

It felt good to be called kind.

"You've got some young visitors," the man said to the old woman. "Why don't we end classes for today?"

"Trying to get out of your arithmetic lesson, Mr. Winchell?" the woman asked. "It won't work. I know where you live."

Mr. Winchell gave a nice little laugh, gathered up
his books, and left the room, giving some of the kids a
friendly pat on the head as he walked by.

Carolyn's big yellow dog shuffled up to the woman
and put his paws on her lap.

"I'm so glad we gave him a bath," Shoshona said.

"What's your dog's name?" the woman asked
Carolyn, who was right there beside him.

"Rosie," Carolyn said, before anyone could say that
she didn't talk. Dayton bent down and tried to get her
to say it again, but she seemed to think that once was
enough.

"My name is Mildred," the woman said. "Rosie,
please get down." Rosie obeyed.

"Are you the governor's mother?" Shoshona asked.

"I am."

"We came to see the governor."

"He's not here."

"We read it in the newspaper," Gitana insisted.
"He's supposed to be here."

"His staff puts those stories out," said Mildred.
"It's nothing to do with me."

"Are you sure he's not coming?" Jake asked. "This
was our one chance to see him."

"I'm certain he won't be here. My son and I have an agreement. He doesn't come to see me, and I stop trying to have him impeached."

"What's impeached?" asked Lydia.

"Fired," answered Gitana.

"Fired with extreme humiliation," Mildred added.

"He doesn't come to see you?" Ricardo asked. "You never see him?"

"I see him on TV. I see him in the newspapers. I hear him on the radio. That's quite enough."

"Don't you miss him?" Manuel asked.

"No, I don't. We can't be together without arguing. We've both tried."

"You're not a good mother," Dayton accused her. "You should love your son. You should look out for him."

"My son is a grown man. If all you're going to do is lecture me on things you know nothing about, I'll get Mr. Winchell back in here to work on his multiplication tables."

Ten pairs of eyes glared at her. Eleven, including Rosie's.

"We'll take her with us," Harlan said.

"What?" Shoshona asked.

"We'll take her with us," Harlan said again. "The governor wants her back, he'll have to give us what we want."

"The governor doesn't like her," Gitana said. "He may not want her back."

"Stop talking like this!" Shoshona said, stepping between them.

"Are you planning to kidnap me?" Mildred asked, looking more amused than alarmed. "That will add some excitement to a dull Sunday. Just how do you propose to smuggle me out of the building?"

"Be quiet," Gitana said. "We need to think."

"You are being disrespectful, young lady. This visit is over." Mildred reached behind her and grabbed a thick metal cane.

The children watched as she struggled to raise herself up.

"She couldn't even make it up the steps," said Lydia. "She's too old and falling apart."

"She might even die," said Ricardo, "right in front of us."

"Quit drooling, you little ghouls," Mildred said, finally on her feet. She was very tall, now that she was standing. "I had a broken hip, I don't have rigor mortis. I've climbed mountains, hiked through the Amazon, and survived thirty-five years in a classroom. I can make it up any set of stairs you can."

"Prove it," said Gitana.

"I'm beyond the age when I need to prove anything to anybody. Give me a reason that might interest me. Are you after money, power, or are you just trying to get back at your mothers and fathers for being bad parents?"

Something in Jake snapped. "Don't talk like that about our parents!" he cried. "Our moms are in prison, but they're good people and should be home with us. But your son won't even answer my letters. I've been writing him for three years, and you didn't teach him to be polite enough to answer his mail. That makes you a bad parent."

"Your mothers are all in prison?" Mildred asked.

"Except for Gitana—it's her grandmother. And for Harlan, it's his aunt. His mother's dead."

"She died in prison," Harlan said. "Not that you care."

"You're a bundle of judgments, aren't you?" Mildred frowned. "Maybe I do care. How did she die? Did another prisoner kill her?"

181

"You'd like to believe that, wouldn't you?" Harlan sneered. "You'd like to believe we're all animals. My mother had pain in her stomach. She complained to the guards but they thought she was faking. She died of a burst appendix. I didn't get to say good-bye, and I didn't get to go to her funeral. My social worker screwed up."

Mildred shook her head. "People make mistakes—," she began.

"People make mistakes WITH US!" Harlan yelled out the last two words.

"That shouting might bring the nurses," Mildred said. "Talk fast. What's my son got to do with this?"

"We want him to pardon our mothers," said Jake.

"And your current plan is to kidnap me and hold me some place until he complies?"

"We really just wanted to talk with him," Shoshona said. "This kidnap thing is new, and we haven't all agreed to it." She threw Harlan and Gitana one of her Queen-of-Pain glares. "We'd like to ask him why he's never answered any of my brother's letters."

"He answered one," Jake said.

"Not really," said Shoshona.

"Do you have it with you?" Mildred asked.

Jake handed Mildred the notebook full of letters.

"Rough copies?" Mildred asked. "Very good." She read through a few of them and said, "You write very well."

No one had ever told Jake that. He felt a little stunned.

"And the response?"

Jake handed it over. It didn't take her long to read it. But then she looked at it and looked at it, shaking her head back and forth. "Some children are such a disappointment."

"So are some parents," Gitana said.

Mildred ignored her. She looked thoughtful for a moment. Then suddenly she said, "How did you get here?"

"Our bus driver was a drunk," Rochelle said. "We had to leave him. Then Shoshona and Harlan drove us."

"In a school bus? Turn the sound up on that television."

Before long, they were all looking at an interview with Mr. Nothing, complaining they'd stolen the bus. Then someone from the church claimed their congregation had been terrorized.

"Those clips have been running all day," said Mildred.

"They're lying," said Shoshona.

"Inaccurate news. Imagine that," said Mildred. "I know where we can find the governor."

"Where?"

Mildred smiled. "It's Mother's Day. He's playing golf."

CHAPTER 15

You'll never get to see him without me,"
Mildred said. "He keeps himself protected."

"We'll have to kidnap you after all," said Gitana
with a grin.

It took some planning to get Mildred away from
Sunnycrest without having to answer a lot of questions.
"They'll probably say I can't leave without another
adult along to help in case I fall," Mildred explained.

"Can't you just walk out?" Jake asked. "You're old.
You should be able to do what you want."

"Thanks—I think," said Mildred, putting on her
jacket. "It has to do with insurance and liability.
Everyone is afraid of being sued."

She recruited Mr. Winchell and some of her other friends to help out. They went to the far end of the hall and faked heart attacks and dizzy spells to keep the nurses occupied and away from the front door. Mildred couldn't move all that fast with her cane, but they got her outside and up the steps of the bus without being stopped.

"It's not far," Mildred said, "but you'd better let me drive."

Shoshona didn't want to give up the wheel. She'd gotten comfortable with driving the bus. Reluctantly, she took the closest seat, not caring that Jake was already in it and had to slide over. "You know how to drive?"

"I drove an ambulance in England during the blitz and a school bus for many years after that. Plus, I have an up-to-date driver's license, which is probably more than you have. Why do young people always think old people are incompetent?"

"Because old people always think young people are," said Gitana.

There wasn't much talking after that. The bus got quiet, but it wasn't the sort of quiet that came before the visit to the prison, or the quiet that came after the crying was done.

It was a quiet that said something important was about to happen.

Jake looked out his window, and when Shoshona put her arm around him, he didn't even mind.

The golf course was just on the other side of town. It was fenced in with barbed wire.

"Devil's rope," said Jake. "To keep the golfers from escaping."

A police car sat at the entrance. Two officers leaned against it.

"Are they for us?" Dayton asked.

"They're for my son," said Mildred. "They help him feel important. I'll talk to them. They'll let us through."

Mildred drove off the highway into the lane that led to the golf course. She braked and slid open the driver's window to talk to the police.

"The golf course is closed today for a private function, ma'am," the officer said.

"Yes, I know. It's the annual Mother's Day Governor's Tournament for Juvenile Diabetes. I'm the governor's mother. He was supposed to leave word with you to let me through."

"I'm sorry, ma'am. We didn't get that message."

"My son was inconsiderate as a teenager, too," Mildred said. Gitana passed her the newspaper photo. "Here you are, Officer. This should be enough for you to let us through."

The officer looked at the photo, scratched his nose, and asked, "Who are these children with you?"

"We're the entertainment." Lydia and Rochelle pushed up to the window, flinging their feather boas in Mildred's face and launching into one of their Pointer Sisters songs.

Shoshona pulled them away from the window. "We're the St. Jude's Children's Choir," she said. Jake was impressed that she could come up with such a good lie on such short notice.

The officer still didn't seem convinced. Jake saw the other cop looking at the bus and talking into his radio.

"How are you honoring your mother today, young man?" Mildred asked him. "Have you called her? Sent her flowers? Are you taking her out to dinner?"

"Go right ahead, ma'am. I'll let them know you're coming." He waved them forward.

"I love guilt," Mildred said, and got the bus moving again.

"I think the other one was checking on us," Jake said.

"Everybody, stay calm," Mildred said. "I'll get you in front of the governor, then you can say what you want to say."

"Are you ready?" Shoshona asked Jake.

"You're going to let me talk?"

"They're your letters," she said. "You'll know what to say."

Jake hesitated. "But what if I get it wrong?"

"You won't."

The lane opened up to a big parking lot and a huge white clubhouse. A crowd was gathered in front of a low stage set up on the grass under a Juvenile Diabetes banner. A tall man was giving a speech. Television cameras and newspaper reporters were standing by.

"The police are here," Dayton said, looking out the rear window of the bus. Two police cars were following them.

"You'll have to move fast," Mildred said. "Let me get off the bus first so the police and my son can see me. Then run as fast as you can up onto that stage."

She parked the bus close to the platform, right on

the grass, forcing part of the crowd to move out of her way.

"We'll stand in a group like a choir," Shoshona said. "We'll tell the governor we have a gift for him. Wear your feathers," she said to Lydia and Rochelle. "They won't be afraid of kids wearing feathers."

"Bring those letters," Gitana told Jake. She picked up the briefcase full of files. "Ready?" Mildred was on her feet. She opened the door and stepped outside. Then she looked over her shoulder. "Everybody, run!"

Everybody ran. The smaller ones slipped through the crowd. The bigger ones pushed their way through. Shoshona shaped them into a group, like a choir, near the center of the stage. Rosie sat obediently beside Carolyn.

The governor, wearing a golfing outfit, froze. Then he plastered a phony smile on his face and helped his mother onto the stage. Mildred's smile was equally phony.

"They *really* don't like each other," Manuel said in a low voice.

Mildred was now at the microphone with her son. The governor introduced her.

"I'm pleased to present to you my mother! Happy

Mother's Day, Mom!"

There was polite applause. Then it was Mildred's turn. She looked serenely out over the audience. "In honor of your excellent work on behalf of Juvenile Diabetes, son, I've brought you these lovely children. They have something to share with you."

Everyone smiled and applauded, even though the children were hardly lovely. They'd been on a bus for two days—nearly three—and looked like it, in spite of Shoshona's efforts.

The governor, the smile still frozen on his face, looked at the group and waited for his gift.

Shoshona tried to push Jake forward. But the governor was taller than he expected, and there were cameras and people in nice clothes, and lots of security standing by. He felt too small and unimportant to say anything.

Rochelle started singing. She'd been coaching Lydia, and the others must have been paying more attention than Jake had, because they joined in. It only took a line or two before Shoshona picked it up, her voice rich and full.

"Sometimes I feel like a motherless child," he heard his sister sing.

The stronger she sang, the stronger Jake felt.

When she got to the verse, "Motherless children have a real hard time," she didn't even cry.

Jake knew what to do.

As the song came to a close, he stepped forward and walked, shaking, to the microphone. He could hear the cameras clicking. He tilted the microphone down so he could speak into it, and said, "My name is Jake. Jacob Tyronne DeShawn."

The governor's eye twitched a little. His smile wasn't quite so big.

"I've been writing to you for three years, ever since my mother was arrested." He held up the notebook. "These are the rough copies."

Jake stopped, not sure what to say next. He looked back at the others. Gitana pointed to the envelope. He turned back to the crowd.

"I want you to pardon my mother out of prison. We all have mothers in Wickham, except for Gitana, who has a grandmother there, and Harlan, who has an aunt. He had a mother there, too, but the prison people killed her."

Still smiling, the governor tried to step up to the microphone. His mother stepped in his way. Jake kept talking.

"I wrote to you so many times, and you only answered once." He couldn't hold the microphone and take the letter out of the envelope, so Mildred did it for him. Then she held the letter up.

"Here's what you wrote, at the top of one of my letters," Jake continued.

Then he said it. "'Get this kid off my back. He must be a nutcase.'"

The photographers clicked their cameras and the television people leaned in closer.

"I'm not a nutcase, Mr. Governor. None of us is, even though our files say we are."

Gitana held up the briefcase.

Jake looked right into the television camera. "We just want our mothers to come home."

That was it. That was all he had to say. He let go of the microphone and waited for the governor to speak.

"Governor, how does this request fit in with your policies on crime?" a reporter asked.

The governor turned his back to the crowd, glared at his mother, glared at Jake, and glared at his aides.

When he turned around again, the glare was gone.

"I am very pleased to finally meet this wonderful

young man—all these wonderful young people—who are living proof of the greatness of my government's commitment to youth services. Criminals must not be coddled! Under my administration, we have gotten tough on crime, and we will continue to be tough on crime! We believe—"

But Jake stopped listening. After three years of writing and waiting and hoping, he had his answer. And the answer was no. He turned his back to the governor and started across the stage, back to the bus kids, back to his friends.

But it wasn't over.

Harlan, his face red with rage, grabbed the briefcase full of lying files out of Gitana's hands. "You're not listening," he yelled. "None of you ever listens, and when you talk, you don't say anything. It's nothing but lies with you people!"

What happened next happened in slow motion. Harlan opened the clasp on the briefcase and stuck his hand inside. But before he could pull out the files, a security officer stepped in front of the governor. Then he drew his gun, and aimed it at Harlan.

He thinks Harlan has a gun, thought Jake.

Jakeman knew what to do. He leapt toward the

security officer on his powerful legs and stretched out his barbed-wire arms to push away the officer's gun.

The bullet hit Jake in the shoulder. He slammed to the ground, and all went dark.

CHAPTER 16

J ake smelled disinfectant. He thought he was back on the bus, but then he opened his eyes. He was in a bed, in a hospital, in a little space with curtains all around.

"Harlan says you're a hero. I think he is right."

Shoshona was sitting beside his bed, holding his hand as if he were a little kid.

His mouth felt full of cotton. "I don't feel like a hero," he managed to say. He hurt all over, not just his shoulder.

"Real heroes never do." Shoshona opened a drinking box of orange juice, stuck a straw into it, and helped Jake sit up to take a drink. "They want you to stay here for a couple of days."

"You're leaving me here? By myself?"

"No one's leaving. We're being put up in the Legion Hall. Sleeping bags on the floor. Church groups bringing in food. People have been nice."

"They're all staying? Even Gitana?"

"No one wanted to leave without you. Especially not Gitana. 'We have to stay together,' she said."

Jake took another drink of juice, then Shoshona put the box on the little tray that was sitting across the bed. "What happened?" he asked.

"You passed out," Shoshona told him. "Shock, they told me. They took the bullet out of your shoulder. You're going to be fine."

I've been shot, Jake thought. It was just like being in a movie. But in a movie, it didn't really hurt. "Did Mom get pardoned?"

"The governor's security men and the police whisked him out of there pretty quick. He didn't have time to pardon anybody." Shoshona laughed. "They tried to take Mildred, too, but she hit them with her cane.

"The reporters covered everything. They talked to all of us, and they got it all on camera."

"And I missed it." Jake sighed.

"They'll interview you when you feel better. None of this would have happened without you," Shoshona said. "I'm sorry I laughed about writing to the governor. And I'm sorry I didn't encourage you more about Jakeman. I took a look at it," she added, holding up his backpack. "It's pretty good." She put the pack on top of the little table beside the bed, where he could easily reach it.

Jake didn't know what was more of a shock—Shoshona apologizing or Shoshona liking his comic book.

A nurse came around the curtain. "I have some pills for Jake to help with his pain, and I have orders for you to leave," she said to Shoshona. "You can come back tomorrow."

Shoshona actually stood up to obey the nurse. Shoshona never obeyed anybody. Before she left, she kissed Jake on the forehead. He was in pain and couldn't stop her, but he didn't really mind.

"Your comic book is good," she said, before leaving. "But the drawing of Carolyn and the cow is really special. Do more like that. Draw our trip. Help us to remember it."

The nurse helped Jake swallow the pills with more orange juice, then he lay back down to wait for the pain to stop.

"Draw our trip," Shoshona had said.

He reached out his hand to touch the strap of his backpack.

He would begin by drawing Shoshona. She'd be behind the wheel of the bus.

And she'd be singing.

Dear Mr. Governor,

This will be the last letter I write to you. Maybe you'll let my mother out of prison. Probably you won't. Shoshona says people only change when they want to change. You seem to like yourself the way you are, and that's too bad, because you're really not nice at all. I know now that you can have a nice life and not think about us at all. That's too bad for you, because we're worth thinking about.

I never thought Shoshona could drive a bus. I never thought we could all take care of each other. I never thought we'd actually get to talk to reporters. Maybe we can do other things I've never thought we could.

So I'm going to say good-bye now. I'm Jakeman and I'm stronger than barbed wire. Maybe I'll run for governor one day and put you out of a job.

Respectfully yours,

Jacob Tyronne DeShawn

About the Author

Deborah Ellis is the internationally acclaimed author of award-winning books for children, including the *Breadwinner* trilogy, *A Company of Fools*, *The Heaven Shop*, and *Our Stories, Our Songs*. A peace activist and humanitarian field worker, Deborah has traveled the world to meet with and hear the stories of children marginalized by poverty, war, and illness. She has been honored with the Governor General's Award, the Jane Addams Children's Book Award, an ALA Notable, the Vicky Metcalf Award for a body of work, and the Children's Africana Book Award Honor Book for Older Readers. Deborah lives in Simcoe, Ontario.

Photo courtesy of Fortunato

OTHER BOOKS
BY DEBORAH ELLIS

Our Stories, Our Songs: African Children Talk About AIDS
978-1-55041-913-9 hardcover
978-1-55041-912-2 paperback

"The authentic details speak of loss, fear, and grief; incredible kindness; and courage, as well as hope for the future. The readable design includes informative boxed insets and quotes, side-by-side with each child's immediate experience. Readers older than the target audience will want this, too, for both the basic information and the heartrending stories."
— *Booklist* starred review

"Every entry is laden with insight, potent with devastating unselfconsciousness...This collection should be part of every child's adolescence, and to my mind, it's a hands-down winner of the Norma Fleck Award for Canadian Children's Non-Fiction." —*Toronto Star*

- American Library Association Notable Children's Book
- Book Links Best Book for the Classroom 2005
- Booklist starred review
- School Library Journal Best Book for 2005
- School Library Journal starred review
- 2006 Information Book Award finalist
- IODE Violet Downey Book Award for 2005 shortlist
- 2006 Norma Fleck Award for Canadian Children's Non-Fiction finalist

The Heaven Shop
978-1-55041-908-5 hardcover
978-1-55041-907-8 paperback

"Deborah Ellis always tackles difficult issues, so *The Heaven Shop*, a powerful and passionate novel about AIDS in Africa, should not surprise her readers. But what is exceptional about Ellis's story is how uncompromising she continues to be... *The Heaven Shop* never gets strident, but it certainly offers readers a clear sense of the helplessness that African children and young adults face in confronting HIV/AIDS. What the novel does best is offer a human face to the child victims. Binti, like Parvana (the heroine of Ellis's *Breadwinner* trilogy) before her, is a plucky, high-spirited heroine whom young readers will take to their hearts... a groundbreaking novel that should be in classroom libraries." —*Quill and Quire*

- Jane Addams Children's Book Award Honour Book
- Ruth and Sylvia Schwartz Children's Book Award for Young Adult/Middle Reader books finalist
- Children's Africana Book Awards (CABA) 2005 Honor Book for Older Readers
- Golden Oak Award finalist 2005
- 2006 Manitoba Young Readers' Choice Award Honour Book
- ForeWord Magazine 2004 Book of the Year Award finalist
- 2006 Rocky Mountain Book Award shortlist
- Canadian Children's Book Centre Our Choice 2005

A Company of Fools
978-1-55041-721-0 paperback

"The voice of Henri, a choir student in the Abbey of St. Luc in 1348, is clear, thoughtful, and sweet as he chronicles the events of the previous year, when the Black Death came to France and when Micah came to the abbey. Brother Bartholomew is always bringing odd things back from his travels, like the muddy stick that became a rose bush, and he brings filthy, noisy Micah too: the boy can sing like an angel. Henri, quiet, bookish, and in love with the order and rule of the abbey, is astonished by Micah, who does as he pleases. Then comes the plague, and Paris is no longer a place of bright wonders. Micah and Henri hatch the idea of singing to cheer the populace, so they become the Company of Fools, providing respite from the constant funeral dirges. What happens to Micah's song, and to Henri, makes a vivid chronicle of monks, good and bad, and intentions, good and bad, set in the horrific context of a plague year. Quicksilver language and strong imagery propel a powerful historical tale." —*Booklist*

- Canadian Library Association Book of the Year
   Honour Book
- Geoffrey Bilson Award for Historical Fiction
   Honour Book
- Ruth Schwartz Award finalist
- Manitoba Young Readers' Choice Award Nominee
- Mr. Christie's Silver Book Award
- Rocky Mountain Book Award Nominee